Bridget looked up at him. "You really don't trust women, do you?" she said quietly.

He shoved his hands into his pockets and looked down at her meditatively. "I don't trust anyone—on face value."

Then you're just as likely not to believe this is your baby—the thought ran through Bridget's mind—*and that would be the* final *insult.*

LINDSAY ARMSTRONG

I was born in South Africa, but I'm an Australian citizen now, with a New Zealand–born husband. We had an epic introduction to Australia. We landed in Perth, then drove around the "top end" with four kids under the age of eight. There were some marvelous times and wonderful sights and ever since, we've been fascinated by wild Australia. We've done quite a bit of exploring the coastline by boat, including one amazing trip to the Kimberley.

We've also farmed and trained racehorses, and after our fifth child was born I started to write. It was something I'd always wanted to do but never seemed to know how to start. Then one day I sat down at the kitchen table with an abandoned exercise book, suddenly convinced the time had come to stop dreaming about it and start doing it. That book never got published, but it certainly opened the floodgates!

ONE NIGHT PREGNANCY

LINDSAY ARMSTRONG

~ Unexpected Babies ~

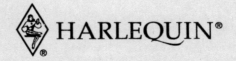

HARLEQUIN®

TORONTO • NEW YORK • LONDON
AMSTERDAM • PARIS • SYDNEY • HAMBURG
STOCKHOLM • ATHENS • TOKYO • MILAN • MADRID
PRAGUE • WARSAW • BUDAPEST • AUCKLAND

Recycling programs
for this product may
not exist in your area.

ISBN-13: 978-0-373-88159-8

ONE NIGHT PREGNANCY

First North American Publication 2010.

www.eHarlequin.com

Printed in U.S.A.

ONE NIGHT PREGNANCY

CHAPTER ONE

IT WAS a filthy night in the Gold Coast hinterland.

It hadn't started out as such, but severe summer storms were not unknown in the area and this series had sped across the escarpment, taking even the weather bureau by surprise. Rain was teeming down, and gusts of wind buffeted Bridget Tully-Smith's car. The ribbon of winding, narrow road between the dark peaks of the Numinbah Valley disappeared regularly as the windscreen wipers squelched back and forth, revealing and concealing.

She'd been staying with a married friend who had a hobby farm and was breeding, of all things, llamas. It had been an enjoyable weekend. Her friend had a young baby, a devoted husband, and their particular patch of the Numinbah Valley was wonderfully rural.

It should have been only an hour's drive back to the Gold Coast, but as the darkness drew in and the storms hit, somehow or other she got lost. Somehow or other she found herself on a secondary road, little more than a track, just as the rain became torrential—as if the heavens above had opened and were literally hell-bent on deluging the area.

Then she came round a bend to a concrete causeway-style bridge, or what had probably been one but was now a raging torrent, cutting the road in two. It came upon her so suddenly she had no choice but to brake sharply—and that very nearly proved to be her undoing.

The back of her car fishtailed, and she felt the tug of the creek water on it, more powerful than the brakes or the handbrake. In perhaps the quickest-thinking moment of her life, she leapt out of the car as the back of it was slowly pushed to midstream, and scrabbled with all her might to attain higher ground.

She found a gravelly hillock supporting a young gum tree, and clung to it as she watched in horrified disbelief. Her car straightened, with its nose pointing upstream and its headlights illuminating the scene, then floated backwards downstream until it was obscured from view.

'I don't believe this,' she whispered shakily to herself. She tensed as above the wind and the drumming rain she heard an engine, and realised a vehicle was coming from the opposite direction—and coming fast.

Did they know the road? Did they think speed would get them over the bridge? Did they have a four-wheel drive? All these questions flashed through her mind, but she knew she couldn't take a risk on any or all of those factors. She must warn them.

She abandoned her tree and ran out into the middle of the road, jumping up and down and waving her arms. She was wearing a red-and-white fine gingham blouse, and she prayed it would stand out—though she knew her loose beige three-quarter-length pedal-pushers would not; they were plastered with mud.

Perhaps nothing, she thought later, would have averted the disaster that then took place. The vehicle was coming too fast. It didn't even brake. But as it hit the torrent raging over the bridge, just as had happened to her car, the back fishtailed, the stream got it, and it too was swept away at a dangerous angle.

Bridget winced and put a hand to her mouth, because she could see faces at the windows of the vehicle, some of them children, and there were childish cries as windows were wound down, one piercing scream. Then the car disappeared from sight.

She sobbed once and forced herself to examine her options, but they were pitifully few—actually she had none, she conceded, other than to try to reach the car on foot. Her mobile phone was sitting in her car...

But another vehicle suddenly appeared around the bend behind her, and this one managed to stop without skidding, well clear of the torrent.

'Oh, thank heavens,' she breathed as she started to run towards it, slipping and slithering up the muddy road.

A man jumped out before she got to it, tall, in jeans and boots and rain jacket.

He got the first words in. 'What the hell's going on? What are you doing out in this?'

Bridget tried to catch her breath, but it was a panting, emotional explanation she gave. She finished by saying passionately, 'There were children in the car! They'd have no hope against a torrent that can wash away cars. Have you got a phone? Mine's in the car. We need to alert—'

He shook his head.

'What kind of a person doesn't have a mobile phone these days?' Bridget demanded thinly. She was feeling thoroughly over-wrought by now.

'I've got a phone. I've got no signal, though. The country's too rugged.'

'Then—' she wiped the rain out of her eyes '—should I drive your car back to get help while you see what you can do here?'

He shook his head.

She jumped up and down in exasperation. 'Don't keep knocking all my suggestions on the head—*why* not?'

The stranger took a very brief moment to examine her sodden, highly emotional pres-ence. 'I'm not—' he began.

'Yes, you are!'

'You wouldn't get through,' he said pre-cisely. 'There's a rock fall, and a washaway over the road a couple of kilometres back. It happened just after I passed.'

He stopped to open the back of the rather

elderly Land Rover he was driving. 'So I'll go and see what I can do.' He pulled out a hank of rope, a knife in a leather holder that he clipped to his belt, a small axe and a waterproof torch.

'Oh, thank heavens— I'll come.'

'Nope. You stay here.'

'Mister!'

He turned to her impatiently. 'The last thing I need is a hysterical slip of a girl to worry about. I only have one waterproof, that I happen to be wearing—'

'What does that matter?' she interrupted. 'I could hardly get wetter! And—' Bridget drew herself up to her full height: five feet two '—I'm not a hysterical slip of a girl! Let's go!'

Had it been doomed from the start, their rescue mission? She sometimes wondered. They certainly gave it their all. But climbing their way downstream beside the swollen creek, in pouring rain, with bushes and small trees whipping in the sudden gusts of wind, was not only heartbreakingly slow, it was exhausting.

It was also bruising and scraping, and before

long, with still no sign of the car or any of its occupants, all her muscles ached.

That might have accounted for her slipping suddenly and getting herself caught up on an old piece of fence line at the edge of the creek. Somehow a piece of wire slipped into the belt loop of her pants, and she couldn't free herself however much she wriggled.

'Take them off!' the man yelled, and flashed his torch behind her. She looked backwards over her shoulder, and nearly died to see a dirty wall of water coming down towards her.

She didn't give it a second thought. She squirmed out of her pants, but the water caught her and she'd have been washed downstream if her companion hadn't leapt in beside her, managed to tie the rope around her waist and somehow drag and half-carry her to relative safety.

'Oh, thank you! You probably saved my life,' she panted.

He didn't reply to that. 'We've got to get higher. Keep going,' he ordered.

She kept going. They both kept going— until, when her lungs and her heart felt like bursting, he finally called a halt.

'Here—in here,' he said, and flashed the torch around. 'Looks like a cave.'

It *was* a cave, with rocky walls, a dirt floor and an overhang overgrown with dripping bushes and grass. Bridget collapsed on the floor.

When her panting had subsided a bit, she said with irony, 'Looks like the rescuers will have to be rescued.'

'It's often the way,' he replied, and set the torch on a ledge of rock.

Bridget sat up and looked around tentatively. She wasn't all that keen on small spaces, but the thought of what lay outside outweighed her tendency towards claustrophobia.

For the first time her partially unclothed state struck her. She looked down at her bare legs, then realised her blouse was torn and showing parts of her blameless pink lace and silk bra. It was also muddy and torn.

She looked up and discovered her rescuer on his knees, looking down at the dripping, twisted, half-clad length of her with a little glint of admiration in his amazing blue eyes— it was the first time she'd noticed them.

But just as she felt like squirming in embarrassment he looked away abruptly and started to undress himself.

She watched him in startled suspended animation as he ripped off his waterproof jacket, then his long-sleeved plaid shirt, revealing a tanned, muscular chest sprinkled with dark hairs and a pair of powerful shoulders. For a moment her eyes rounded in admiration of her own, then she swallowed with a strange little squawk of sound—a squawk of unwitting apprehension.

He said, matter-of-factly, 'I'm Adam, by the way. Why don't you take your blouse off and put my shirt on? It's relatively dry. I'll look the other way.' He tossed the shirt into her lap and did as he'd promised.

Bridget fingered the shirt. It *was* mostly dry, and it emitted a reassuringly masculine odour of sweat and cotton. It would be heaven—not only as a cover for the deficiencies of her attire, but also because she was starting to shiver with cold.

She pulled her blouse off, and her soaked bra, and slipped into his shirt as quickly as possible, buttoning it with shaky fingers. It was way too big for her, but although the sleeves hung over her hands, the length made her feel at least halfway decent. 'Thank you. Thank you! But will you be all right? I'm decent, incidentally.'

He turned back and pulled his rain jacket on again. 'I'll be fine.' He sat down. 'Not going to return the compliment namewise?'

'Oh, yes! I'm Bridget Smith.' She often used only the second half of her famous double-barrelled surname. 'Oh, no!' She put her hand to her mouth and her eyes darkened with concern as, for the first time since the car with the children had been washed away, she thought suddenly of her own plight. 'My car!'

'Your car will be found,' he said. 'I'm not sure in what condition, but once the waters recede—and they will—it will be somewhere.'

'Do you really think so? My windows were all closed but I didn't have time to lock it—my whole life is in my car!' she said, on a suddenly urgent little note.

He raised an eyebrow at her.

'My phone, my credit cards, my driver's licence, my keys, my Medicare card, not to mention the car itself.' She stopped helplessly.

'They can all be replaced or, in the case of credit cards, stopped.'

Bridget subsided, but her expression remained doomed.

'I take it it's Miss Smith?' he queried.

She shrugged. 'Not necessarily.' Her thoughts returned to her car.

'You're not wearing a wedding ring,' he pointed out.

Bridget hesitated, and stopped looking down the barrel of the chaos in her life if she didn't retrieve her car to look rather intently at the man she was trapped in a cave with.

Then she fished beneath his plaid shirt and pulled out the gold chain she wore around her neck. There was a plain gold wedding ring threaded onto it.

'I see—but why don't you wear it on your finger?' he queried.

Bridget blinked, and wondered how she could assess this man. Because, however good-looking, beautifully built and strong he was, the fact remained that she didn't know him—and one could never be too careful, could one? So it mightn't be a bad idea to have a husband in the wings...

'I've lost a bit of weight and it's just a little big.' The last part was true enough.

'So what's he like? Mr Smith?'

Was it just a casual query? Bridget wondered. To take her mind off the traumatic events surrounding them? Or had he doubted her?

'Actually, he's rather lovely, as Mr Smiths go,' she said lightly, and it was the invention flowing off her tongue so smoothly that caused her to smile appreciatively—not, she thought swiftly, that he would know it. 'He's tall, probably even a bit taller than you,' she continued. 'And he strips to great advantage.' She stopped and asked herself where the hell that particular phrase had sprung to her mind from? A Regency novel? 'Uh…' She soldiered on. 'And of course he's devoted to me.'

'Of course.' A smile appeared fleetingly in those smoky blue eyes—a smile of genuine amusement that, all the same, made her uneasy for some reason. 'Does that mean to say,' he went on, 'he's waiting for you? At home, perhaps?'

'Oh, definitely,' Bridget lied with abandon.

'That's comforting to know. So when you

don't show up, and you don't ring, he's liable to call the police, who in turn are liable to get onto the Emergency Services when they realise *you're* liable to be caught up in this situation?'

'Ah.' A tinge of pink coloured Bridget's dirty cheeks. 'Well, no. Not exactly. I was speaking more generally. He's—he's out of town at the moment. But only on a business trip—and—and—he'll be home tomorrow. Definitely. Or maybe the next day.'

Adam studied her. Her short cap of hair was a coppery bronze, and not even an extremely arduous hike through rocky, sodden terrain had been able to dim her sparkling green eyes, he reflected, and smiled inwardly. They were also very revealing eyes, and from the turmoil they'd revealed as a variety of emotions had chased through them he was fairly sure she was lying. But if she'd chosen to invent a husband, *why* had she?

He narrowed his eyes on the obvious answer. Never trust strange men. Of course. So Bridget Smith was a cautious girl, even on a night like tonight. Well, he'd go along with it if it made her feel safer...

'But hang on!' Bridget stopped looking

guilty. 'The friends I was staying with—they'll probably worry and try to ring me. They wanted me to stay overnight, but I've got an early start tomorrow so...' She looked rueful. 'They might alert someone when they can't get me.'

'OK.' He shrugged and got to his knees. 'I'm going out to reconnoitre. If the water's still rising we may have to move again.'

The water *was* still rising, but not quite as fast.

'I think we can relax for a bit,' he said as he crawled back into the cave. 'The fact that it's not rising so fast may mean it's going to start falling soon.'

Bridget heaved a relieved sigh, but her relief was to be short-lived because there was an almighty crack of sound and something—a tree, they realised moments later—fell down the hillside from above, blocking the entrance to the cave.

She turned convulsively to Adam, her eyes wide and dark with fear. 'We're trapped,' she whispered.

'Trapped? Me?' he replied with a ghost of a smile. 'Don't you believe it, Mrs Smith.'

'But all you have is a small axe and a knife!' she objected.

'You'd be amazed at what I can do with 'em.'

'Are you—are you an axeman?' Bridget asked. 'Like those wood-chopping men you see at country shows?'

For some reason this question seemed to take him by surprise. Then his wide-eyed look was replaced by one of ironic amusement, and he responded with a question of his own. 'Do I look like one?'

'Not really. You look like—well, you could be anything.' She smiled anxiously. 'I didn't mean to be offensive—I think I'll just shut up.'

'Might be a good idea to save our breath,' he murmured, 'for what lies ahead. But, really, you have no need to worry about me. Nor would Mr Smith.'

'Thank you,' she said, but there was a question mark in those green eyes. As if she suspected she was being teased.

He waited for her to retaliate, but she dropped her lashes suddenly and folded her hands primly in her lap.

He was tempted to laugh, but reminded

himself in time that, despite his assurance to the contrary, they *were* actually trapped in a cave by a tree at the moment.

An hour later they were free.

An hour during which Adam had used a combination of pure strength, some chopping, some manipulation with his rope, some propping with rocks and the sturdy axe to move the tree.

'I don't know how you did it!' Bridget gasped as the tree rolled away. 'You're actually amazing!'

'Leverage,' he replied, 'is what's amazing. One should always have a good understanding of levers and leverage.'

'I'll certainly put that on my list of things to learn—oh!' He'd swung the torch over the view from the mouth of the cave, and it wasn't a reassuring sight.

'Yes,' he agreed grimly. 'The water's still rising. OK, Bridget, we need to get out and up as fast as we can. Put the rope around your waist. That way we'll stay together. I'll go first. Ready?'

She nodded.

* * *

The next interlude, and Bridget had no idea how long it took, was sheer torture. The land above the cave rose steeply and was strewn with rocks. It was also slippery, but she followed Adam up the hillside doggedly, although at times it was a one step forward, two steps back kind of progress.

At one point she had to stop because of a burning stitch in her side, and she fell over once. Only the rope stopped her from cartwheeling down the incline.

Fortunately they were level with each other, and she caught sight out of the corner of her eye, during the regular sweep of his torch, of a rock he didn't see. A rock that looked to be teetering dangerously, directly above them. With a high-pitched yell, she cannoned into him, catching him off-balance and pushing him with all her might. They rolled away only inches from where the rock passed on its deadly way down the hillside.

Just as she felt she could go no further, they reached some flat ground, a grassy little plateau, and another sweep of the torch revealed a shed below the hillside, at the far end of it.

'Oh, thank heavens,' she breathed, but

sank to her knees in utter exhaustion. 'I just need—a—little break, though. Not long,' she assured her companion, her voice coming in great gasps.

He came to stand over her and shone the torch down on her. She couldn't read his expression. She couldn't actually think straight, she just did as she was told.

'You hold this,' he said, and gave her the torch. She took it, and was completely unprepared to be hoisted to her feet and then up into his arms.

'But—but—what are you doing?' she stammered as he started to walk. 'I really—'

'Shut up, Mrs Smith,' he recommended. 'You've actually been rather amazing yourself, and you probably saved *my* life. It's the least I can do. Would you mind directing the torchlight forward?'

Bridget hastily repositioned the torch so he could see where he was going, and unwittingly began to relax. More than that, she had to admit to herself that it was heaven. His arms felt amazingly strong; she felt amazingly safe. And she had seriously to doubt she could have covered the remaining ground on her own two feet, because she felt as weak as a kitten.

They reached the shed.

'It's locked,' he said as he put her down. 'But on a night like tonight, and since we're not here to rob anyone, I don't suppose they'd mind if we do this.' And with a single stroke of the axe, pulled from his belt, he broke the padlock.

'Yes, well.' Bridget blinked a little dazedly. 'You're probably right. And we can always replace things.'

He looked down at her with a faint smile. 'We can, indeed. After you, ma'am.'

Bridget shuffled into the shed and made a sound of heartfelt approval at what she saw. In fact she discovered herself to be feeling a lot less sandbagged as she looked around.

It was an old shed, and didn't look particularly solid, but there were bales of straw stacked high against one wall, a double bed against another. There were some paraffin lamps, hanging on hooks, a kettle and a primus stove, some chipped mugs and a tea caddy standing on an upturned tea chest. There were racks of neatly sorted horse gear: headstalls, bridles, saddles and brushes. Three old thin towels hung on a railing, along with two light horse rugs.

There was also a wood-burning stove, with a chimney going through the roof. It was packed with paper and billets of wood.

'Glory be,' Adam remarked. He raised his voice against the drumming of rain on the tin roof. 'In these conditions you could call this place the Numinbah Hilton.'

Bridget chuckled. Then she sobered. 'Those children—' she began.

'Bridget.' He turned to look down at her. 'We did our best. It's a small miracle we weren't drowned in the process. They will be fine, riding it out somehow. Just hold onto that thought.'

'But I was wondering—there must be a road to here, and maybe we could go for help.'

'I had the same thought,' he said. 'Do you have any idea where we are?'

'Well, no, but—'

'Neither do I,' he broke in. 'In fact I'm thoroughly disorientated after all the twists and turns that creek took. We could get even more hopelessly lost, whereas in the daylight this could be a good point of reference. We may even be able to flag a passing helicopter.

There's bound to be some State Emergency Services scouting the area after a storm like this. But, listen, just in case there's a house attached to this paddock and shed, I am going to scout around a bit. As for you—' he scanned the dirty, sopping length of her '—first of all, do you have any sprains, strains, fractures or the like?'

Her eyes widened. 'No, I don't think so. Just a few bruises and scrapes.'

'OK—now, you may not approve of this suggestion, but it's an order, actually, and you can hold it against me as much as you like.' For a moment there was a rather mercilessly teasing glint in his eyes.

She stiffened her spine against that glint. 'What order?' she asked with hauteur.

He studied her tilted chin and smiled briefly. 'I don't know if you noticed a tank at the corner of the shed, collecting rainwater from the roof?'

She shook her head.

'Well, it's there, and it's overflowing. After I've gone, go out, take your clothes off, and stand under the overflow pipe. Wash all the mud, blood and whatever off yourself, then stand under the water for a couple of minutes.

Do your bruises a world of good. But I'll get the fire going first.' He turned away.

'I—' she started to say mutinously.

'Bridget,' he returned dangerously over his shoulder, 'don't argue.'

'But I've got nothing to wear!'

'Yes, you have.' He pointed to one of the railings. 'You can wrap yourself in one of those horse rugs.'

He did get the fire *and* three paraffin lamps going before he left.

'Take care,' she said. 'I—I'm not too keen about being left on my own here. Naturally I wouldn't want anything to happen to you, either.' She grimaced. 'That sounds like an afterthought if ever I heard one! But I do mean it.'

He inclined his head and hid the smile in his eyes. 'Thank you. I won't be going too far. Not only because I don't want to get lost, but also because I don't want the torch to run out on me.' He touched her casually on the cheek with his fingertips. 'You take care too.'

She watched him walk out of the shed into the rainswept night and swallowed back the cry that rose in her throat—the urge to tell him she'd go with him. Swallowed it because she knew that her brief resurgence of energy, such as it was, would not survive.

So she forced herself to examine his suggestion—or order. She looked down at herself. She was a mess of mud, his shirt was caked with it, and below her legs were liberally streaked with it.

It made sense, in other words, to get clean. If only she had something else to wear afterwards other than a horse rug...

It was like the answer to a prayer. Some instinct prompted her to look under the pillows on the bed, and she discovered a clean pair of yellow flannelette pyjamas patterned with blue teddy bears.

Under the second pillow was a pair of men's tracksuit pants and a white T-shirt.

'You beauty!' she breathed. 'Not only can I be comfortable overnight, but I won't have to be rescued wearing a horse rug. And not only *that*, my fellow traveller can be decent and dry too—which is important, I'm sure. OK. Onward to the shower, Mrs Smith!' And she marched out of the shed.

It was a weird experience, showering beneath an overflow pipe in the middle of the night, in the middle of a deluge, in the altogether, even though there was a brief lull in the rain.

She took a lamp with her, and found a hook on the shed wall for it. It illuminated the scene, and she could see a huge gum tree on the hill behind the shed, plus the ruins of some old stone structure.

Definitely weird, she decided as the water streamed down her body, and freezing as well. But at least the tank stood on a concrete pad, and there was a concrete path to it from the shed door. She'd also discovered a bucket tucked behind the tank, with a piece of soap and a nailbrush in it.

Did someone make a habit of showering from the rainwater tank? she wondered. Not that it would always be overflowing, but it had a tap. Maybe they filled the bucket from the tap and poured it over themselves?

She didn't stay around much longer to ponder the mysteries of the rainwater tank, but skipped inside and dried herself off in front of the fire. Then she examined herself, and, satisfied she would find no serious cuts, donned the teddy bear pyjamas.

'Sorry,' she murmured to the owner of the pyjamas. 'I'll get you a new pair!'

And then she turned her attention to the primus stove and the possibility—the heavenly possibility—of making a cup of tea.

Adam came back just as she was sipping strong black tea from one of the chipped mugs.

'I've just made some tea. I'll get you some. Any luck?'

He peeled off his waterproof. 'No—where did you get those?' He eyed the yellow pyjamas patterned with blue teddy bears.

She explained, and pointed out the track pants and T-shirt. 'You know, I can't help wondering if someone lives here at times.' She poured bubbling water onto a teabag in the second mug and handed it to him.

'I think you could be right—thanks. There's no house nearby, but there's evidence of some foundations. They're probably using the shed while they build the house. The driveway leads to a dirt road—it's now deep mud—with a locked gate.'

'There may be horses out there—maybe fenced in.'

'I hope there are, so long as they're safe. The owners may come to check them out.' He put his cup down. 'You obviously took up my suggestion?' He inspected her clean, shiny face.

'I thought it was an order.'

His lips twisted. 'What was it like?'

'Weird,' she said with feeling. 'But if I could do it, so could you.'

'Just going, Mrs Smith,' he murmured.

Bridget watched the shed door close behind him and found herself standing in the same spot, still staring at the door a good minute later, as she visualised the man called Adam showering as she had done beneath the rain-water tank overflow. It was not hard to visualise his powerful body naked, that fine physique sleek with water...

She blushed suddenly, and moved precipitately—only to trip. She righted herself and castigated herself mentally. Anyone would think she was a silly, starstruck schoolgirl! All right, yes, she might have come out in sudden goosebumps, but at twenty-three surely she had the maturity to recognise it as a purely physical reaction to a dangerously attractive man? Besides which, she was allergic to dangerously attractive men who turned out to be less than likeable— wasn't she?

All the same, when Adam came back from showering wrapped in a towel, and she turned away while he dried himself in front of the fire and donned the track pants and T-shirt, she was aware of him again in her mind's eye. In a way that again raised goosebumps on her skin and caused her to feel a little hot.

Stop it, Bridget, she commanded herself.

An hour or so later another heavy storm broke overhead.

It was close to midnight.

Adam and Bridget were dozing side by side on the double bed when lightning illuminated the shed and a boom of thunder reverberated directly overhead, or so it seemed. Bridget woke and rolled towards Adam with a little cry of fear. He put his arms around her, but she started to shake with barely suppressed sobs.

'It's only another storm,' he said, and stroked her hair.

'I know,' she wept, 'but haven't we been through enough? And I can't stop thinking about those kids out there in this!'

'Hush... Listen, I'm going to put some more wood on the fire. Then I'll be right back.'

He was as good as his word, and when he came back, as if it was the most natural thing in the world, he piled the pillows up behind them and pulled her loosely into his arms. 'Tell me about yourself, Bridget. What do you do? Where were you born? What do your parents do?'

'I work in a television newsroom. At the moment I'm everyone's gofer, but I'm hoping for better things.'

She shuddered as another crack of thunder tore the night but soldiered on.

'I was born in Brisbane. My father died in an accident a few years ago, and my mother has remarried. She lives overseas at the moment. I did a BA at Queensland University, majoring in journalism. My father was a journalist, so I guess that's where I get it from.' She paused to consider for a moment.

She did enjoy her job, but *had* she inherited her father's passion for journalism? She sometimes stopped to wonder whether it had been her admiration for her father that had moved her to pursue the same career rather than a deep, abiding feel for it. She often found herself feeling restless, and as if she'd prefer to be doing something else—but what?

Adam broke the silence and the train of her thoughts.

'Now for the question of Mr Smith.' He looked at her with suspicious gravity.

Bridget bit her lip. 'There is no Mr Smith. The ring...' She fingered the chain around her neck. 'It's my mother's, but since I didn't know you, it seemed a good idea to invent a husband.'

'I wondered about that.'

'Why? I mean how could you tell I was lying?'

He considered. 'You have very revealing eyes. It also sounded like pure invention.'

Bridget blushed faintly.

He traced the outline of her chin lightly. 'So, no romantic involvement at the moment?'

Perhaps it was the storm raging overhead, perhaps it was the reassuring warmth of his proximity, but for whatever reason Bridget found herself telling Adam things she'd not told another soul. Things to do with how she had fallen madly in love at twenty-one, how it had led to an affair—a first for her—and how it had been a disaster.

'He changed,' she said sadly. 'He became possessive, and yet...' she paused '...oddly critical of me. But that was probably because I didn't—well—I didn't seem to be very good at sex. I think a lot of that was to do with the fact that I would really rather have waited—until we'd got engaged at least.'

She heaved a heartfelt sigh and continued. 'I—it didn't take that long for me to discover I'd gone to bed with a man I didn't seem to like much. Oh, he was good-looking, and fun to be with, but…' She trailed off. 'He became rather scary when I broke it off.' She shrugged. 'All of which amounts to the fact that I haven't tried again—I don't know why I'm telling you all this.' She looked into Adam's blue eyes, now thoroughly red-faced.

'Maybe it needed to be told?' he suggested, and stroked her hair. Creep, he thought at the same time, but didn't say it. He did say, 'Things could be quite different with the right man.'

Bridget looked unconvinced, but didn't pursue it. 'Why did I talk about it now, though?'

He stretched out his legs and pulled the one blanket around them. 'It's been quite a night.

Fear, stress, physical exertion, highs and lows, and now an almighty electrical storm.'

It's more than that, Bridget thought. There's something about this man that really appeals to me. He not only makes me feel safe, he makes me feel interested in him, as if I really want to get to know him and—

She stopped her thoughts there. And what? She was very conscious of him physically, she answered herself, and she just couldn't seem to help herself. Alive to all sorts of little things—like his hands. I love his hands, she decided suddenly. And the way his eyes can laugh, the way his hair falls in his eyes sometimes.

'Not only that,' he went on, and took his hand from her hair to rub his jaw ruefully, 'what it makes you, Mrs Smith, is simply very human. We all make mistakes and some dodgy judgements.'

Bridget thought for a moment, then said, 'I guess so.'

He grimaced at the lack of conviction in her voice. 'But there must be more to Bridget Smith.' He raised his voice as the thunder growled overhead. 'Tell me about your likes and dislikes. What makes you tick?'

'I'm very ordinary.' She paused and cast him a suddenly mischievous little look. 'Well, I do a lot of things fairly competently, but to date nothing outstandingly—although I'm living in hope that my true forte is still to make itself known.'

He laughed. 'What about all the things you do fairly well?'

'Let's see. I paint—at one stage I thought I might be the next Margaret Olley, as I love painting flowers, but not so. I also like doing landscapes. I play the piano, but any hopes I would be the next Eileen Joyce were dashed early on. Mind you, I still enjoy doing both. I once thought I'd like to be a landscape gardener. My parents had a few acres and I loved pottering around the garden.'

She paused and thought. 'And I ride—I love horses. I don't have any of my own, although I did have a couple of ponies as a kid, and I help out at a riding school for disabled children. I seem to have a rapport with kids. Uh…I read all the time, I enjoy cooking, I enjoy being at home and pottering—oh, and I sing.'

'Professionally?' he queried.

She shook her head, her eyes dancing. 'No. I did believe I might be the next Sarah

Brightman, but again not so. That doesn't stop me from singing in the shower and anywhere else I can manage it.'

'Sing for me.'

'Now?'

'Why not?'

So she sang a couple of bars of 'Memory', from *Cats*, in her light, sweet soprano. When she'd finished she confessed she was mad about musicals.

'You sound like a pretty well-rounded girl to me,' he said, with a ghost of a smile still lurking on his lips. 'In days gone by you would have had all the qualifications to be a genteel wife and mother.'

'That sounds really—unexciting,' she said with a gurgle of laughter. 'But it's probably in line with what one of my teachers told me. She said to me, *"You're not going to set the world on fire academically, Bridget, but you are a thoroughly nice girl."'* She looked comically heavenwards. 'Unexciting, or what?'

'Oh, I don't know.' He grinned, and dropped a kiss on her forehead. 'It's nice to be nice, and I think you *are* nice.'

Bridget smiled back at him, unexpectedly warmed. Then a twinkle of humour lit her eyes. 'I showed her I wasn't such a disaster academically when I got to uni, and I got honours in a couple of subjects, but enough about me—tell me about you?'

His chiselled lips twisted. 'I wouldn't know where to begin.'

'Well, how old are you and where were you born? What do you do? That kind of thing.'

'I'm thirty-one—whereas you would be... twenty-two?'

'Twenty-three.'

'Twenty-three,' he repeated. 'I was born in Sydney. I've done many things. I'm also pretty keen on horses, but—' he raised his eyebrows '—since you ask, I'm something of a rolling stone.'

'You mean—no ties?' she hazarded.

'No ties,' he agreed.

'Did you get your fingers burnt by a woman once?'

For some reason that quiet question, uttered with a mix of wisdom and compassion, caught his attention fairly and squarely, and his remarkable blue gaze rested on Bridget thoughtfully for a long moment. 'You could say so.'

'Would you like to tell me?'

A little jolt of laughter shook him. 'No.'

Bridget faced him expressionlessly. Her hair had dried to a silky cap of copper-gold, brought to life by the firelight. Her eyes were greener in that same firelight. And, while the teddy bear pyjamas made her look about sixteen, there was, as the man called Adam knew, a perfect little figure beneath them, with high breasts, hips like perfect fruit and a slender waist.

She was also, he reflected, brave.

And no fool, he discovered, when she said, repeating what he'd said to her, 'But maybe it needs to be told?'

He pushed the blanket away and sat up beside her. The thunder was still growling, but it seemed to be moving away. The rain was still falling, but it was much lighter now. How did I get myself into this? he found himself wondering, and looked around somewhat ruefully, then down at the borrowed track pants and T-shirt he was wearing.

'I don't shock easily,' Bridget murmured. 'Did she run away with another man?'

He stared at her, and a muscle flickered in his jaw. Then he smiled, a wry little smile that didn't touch his eyes. 'How did you guess?'

'Well, with a woman involved, that's often how it goes. However…' Bridget paused, and wrinkled her brow. 'He must have had a lot more than you to offer *materially*, otherwise she must have been crazy!'

'Why?'

Bridget blinked and blushed. Then she grimaced inwardly and acknowledged that she'd allowed her tongue to run away with her. So, how to retrieve the situation with minimum embarrassment? Maybe just the truth…?

'You're pretty good-looking, you know. Not only that, you're amazingly resourceful, you're strong, and I couldn't think of anyone I would feel safer with.'

'Thank you,' Adam said gravely. 'None of that was enough to hold her, however. Although I have to admit the competition was quite stiff.'

Bridget frowned. 'But that makes her somewhat suspect, I would say, and maybe not worthy of too much regret?'

He waited impassively, and she tilted her head to one side enquiringly at him. Then he said, 'Have you quite finished, Mrs Smith?'

Bridget immediately looked immensely contrite. 'I'm so sorry,' she said softly. 'It still hurts a lot, I guess? Shall we change the subject?'

Adam swore as he rolled off the bed and went to put the kettle on the stove.

Bridget watched from the bed as he rinsed the mugs in a bucket. The paraffin lamplight softened the outlines of the piled-high bales of straw, but didn't pierce all the shadows in the shed. At least the worst of the storm had definitely moved away.

He spooned instant coffee into the cups and poured the boiling water in. 'Sugar?'

'One, thank you.' She hesitated. 'Look, I *am* sorry. I must have sounded unforgivably nosy.'

He shrugged and handed her a mug, then sat down on the floor beside the bed so he could lean back against it. 'At least it took your mind off the storm.'

'Yes. And I did tell you my life story, so I suppose I was expecting something in return. We also saved each other's lives.'

There was silence, apart from the crackle of the stove and the now faraway thunder.

'She threw me over for my older brother,' he said. 'You're right. She's not worth it. But she—' He broke off. 'My brother is another matter, and one day he'll get his come-up-pance.' He took a sip of coffee. 'Just a matter of finding the right lever.'

Bridget stared at his profile, her eyes wide and horrified—it looked as if it was carved in stone. She swallowed and said the only thing she could think of. 'You're hot on levers, aren't you?' Then, 'I don't think that's a very good idea. Much better for you to move on and—'

'Leave it, Bridget,' he warned, and flicked her a moody blue glance. 'Finish your coffee.'

'OK, I'm sorry,' she said contritely, and drank her coffee in silence.

He took the cup from her and placed it along with his on a ledge beside the bed. Then he climbed back in and took her in his arms again. 'Go to sleep,' he said, not unkindly.

Bridget relaxed and thought how good it felt. How reassuring, how warm and comfortable and natural, and she started to doze off.

Adam, on the other hand, found himself watching her in the firelight and wondering what it was about this girl that had prompted him to tell her things he'd never told anyone else.

Because she was entirely unthreatening? Because she had no idea who he was? Yes, but there was more to it than that. Rather, there was more to his feelings on the subject of Bridget Smith, spinster, he thought wryly.

He felt protective of her, and he had to admire the way she'd slogged through everything nature had thrown at them, but, again, there was more.

As he watched her, he found himself wondering what it would be like to make love to her. To part those pretty pink lips that were twitching a little as she dozed—what was she dreaming of?—and kiss her. What expressions would chase through her green eyes if he, very slowly and gently, initiated her into the pleasures of sex and wiped out the memories some oaf had left her with?

It would be no penance, he realised, and he felt his body stir. It would be the opposite. She felt as if she'd been made to fit into his arms, as if that tender little body should be his property...

Then her eyelashes lifted, taking him by surprise, and for a long frozen moment they stared into each other's eyes. He held his breath as the expression in those green eyes became an incredulous query, as if she'd divined his thoughts.

But it was gone almost immediately, that expression, dismissed with the faintest shake of her head, as if she'd banished it to the realm of the impossible or as if it was a dream, and she fell asleep again.

He released his breath slowly and smiled dryly.

No, it would not be impossible, Bridget Smith, he thought, and nor was it a dream. But it was not going to happen. For a whole host of reasons.

He lay for a while, listening to the rain on the roof, deliberately concentrating on it, and on the fact that it seemed to be getting lighter. But in fact the night hadn't finished with them...

CHAPTER TWO

AT ABOUT three o'clock Bridget woke, and this time Adam was asleep. She was still loosely cuddled in his arms, and there was a faint glow of firelight coming from the stove.

He looked younger, more approachable, but she paused and frowned as she drank his features in. A memory came to her. Could this man possibly have been watching her with desire in his eyes while he'd held her in his arms?

In this bed? In this shed, perhaps?

A little tremor ran through her. Had she imagined it or had she dreamt it? Even if she had, it filled her with a dizzying sense of delight to think of it.

But she put her hand to her mouth in a sudden gesture of concern. How could she feel this way so out of the blue, and about a man she barely knew?

Not only that, but a man who had made no bones about himself—he was a rolling stone, he was anti-commitment, and he had a score to settle over a woman.

Her eyes widened as she realized it didn't seem to make the slightest difference. She still got goosebumps, she still felt those delicious tremors just to think that he might want her...

But would she be any good at it? she wondered. She'd certainly never felt like this before.

Half an hour later she knew she had to pay a visit to the outside toilet, much as she wished otherwise.

It was raining again, so she put on Adam's rain jacket, which covered her voluminously, and unhooked a lamp.

It was when her mission was accomplished and she was scurrying back to the shed that she came to grief—courtesy the mud and Adam's jacket. She tripped on the edge of the jacket at the same time as there was an ominous crack—the kind of crack she'd heard before, earlier in the night. She fell over in the mud and the source of the crack—a branch of the gum tree from the hill behind the shed—rolled down on top of her, bringing with it a smothering shroud of debris.

She got such a fright she blacked out for a couple of moments, and when she came to she couldn't see anything. The tentacles of hysteria started to claim her, and claustrophobia kicked in.

'Bridget, are you all right?' Adam called urgently. 'Bridget, answer me!'

She wriggled a bit. Nothing seemed to hurt desperately but... 'I seem to be pinned around my waist. I can move my legs, but I can't get out—oh, no,' she cried, as there was another crack and more rubble cascaded down the hillside.

'Bridget—Bridget, listen to me,' he instructed. 'Protect your head with your arms, if you can, while I get you out. Try not to move. I *will* get you out, believe me.'

But she didn't believe him, even as she heard chopping and sawing noises, even though she knew there would be more tools in the shed he could use, even though she'd seen what he'd done to another tree. That one had been much smaller...

There was something about being trapped that seemed to convince her she was going to die under the weight of all the rubble the hillside could rain down on her—including, she suddenly remembered, the ruins of the old building she'd seen while showering under the rainwater tank.

For a terrible moment even her legs wouldn't move, she couldn't feel them, and she all but convinced herself she must have broken her back. Later she was to realise it was hysterical paralysis, but at the time her life started to unfold itself in front of her. During the half-hour it took Adam to release her she became more and more convinced this dreadful night was finally going to claim her.

Her ridiculously short life, with no goals achieved, rolled before her eyes. Nothing much of importance to report at all, she thought groggily, and tears flowed down her cheeks.

She didn't immediately believe she was free, until Adam scooped her up in his arms and carried her into the shed.

'Am I dreaming? Is this heaven? Or the other place?' she asked dazedly.

He didn't answer, but put her gently down on the bed. Then he said, 'I'm going to undress you and assess any damage there may be. Try not to make a fuss.'

Bridget heard herself laugh huskily. 'I don't think I'm capable of making a fuss. I got such a fright—I thought I was going to die.'

Adam turned away and put the kettle on the stove. Then he turned back and pulled off the rain jacket and the sodden, torn pyjamas with as much clinical precision as he was capable of. He tested her limbs and her ribs. And when he was assured nothing was broken or twisted he told her she extremely lucky.

Bridget bore it all in silence, even when he filled a bucket with warm water and washed her. She was still grappling with the horrible feeling that she'd been about to die.

She hadn't noticed that he'd warmed one of the towels in front of the stove until he wrapped her in it and put her under the blanket.

She slipped her hand under her cheek and stared unseeingly into the shadows.

Adam gazed down at her for a long moment,

then turned away to load the last of the wood into the stove. She had been extremely lucky, he thought to himself.

The strong PVC material of the rain jacket, even while it had actually become impaled on a sharp piece of wood and trapped her as much as the branch had, had also protected her from the debris. And the branch that had come down on her had had a slight bow in it, which had landed above her waist—thereby pinning her, but not crushing her. All the rocks that had come with it had miraculously missed her, although the other debris—leaves, twigs, grass and earth—had almost smothered her.

He looked down at himself. Once again he was a torn muddy mess, so he stripped, washed himself economically, then wound a towel round his waist. He doused the lamps, as the fire in the stove still roared and provided some light, and climbed into the bed beside her.

She didn't resist when he pulled her gently into his arms. If anything she sighed with relief, and he felt her relax slowly.

Finally she said, as their bodies touched, 'Thank you so much.'

'It was my pleasure,' he answered, with a wry twist to his lips. 'Go to sleep if you can.'

She did drift into an uneasy slumber for a while, but then she woke, shaking and obviously distressed, and suffering a reaction.

'Bridget—Bridget,' he said softly. 'You're safe.'

But she moved jerkily in his arms.

'Hey,' he added, 'it's me—Adam. Your axeman and wood-chopper. Remember?'

Her green eyes focused slowly and she started to relax. 'Oh, thank heavens,' she breathed. 'I thought I was out there again, with things falling down on me and suffocating me.'

'No. I have you in my arms. We're in bed in the shed—remember the shed?—and although the elements are playing havoc outside—' he paused to grimace as another storm cell erupted overhead '—we're warm and dry.'

But she grew anxious again. 'Is that more thunder and lightning? When is it going to stop?' she asked tearfully.

Adam studied her face in the dim light and felt that protective urge run through him again. She'd been through so much, and had borne most of it with a mixture of composure and humour, he thought. But how to comfort her now? More talk?

It came to him that there was only one way he wanted to comfort her—and the thought translated itself instinctively. He pulled her closer and ran his hands over her body.

She stilled, and her lips parted as her eyes grew uncertain, mirroring all her doubts. Was she dreaming again? And, if she wasn't, was she going to be any good at this?

And Adam discovered he couldn't help himself. He lowered his head to kiss her, with the express intention of not only comforting her but at the same time chasing away that look of uncertainty, proving to her she was infinitely desirable.

Bridget remained quite still in his arms for a long moment, then she seemed to melt against him and her lips parted softly beneath his.

Not only did she accept his kiss, but her senses flowered and brought her to a tingling awareness of his body against hers. And as that translated to a wave of desire for him, up and down the length of her, she felt soft and pliant. She felt as if none of her bruises or scrapes even existed, as if it would be the most natural, lovely thing in the world to open her legs and receive him.

And as all hell broke loose above them again, as thunder ricocheted around the ether and lightning flashed sparks of light through the old shed's dirty, high windows, they came together in the timeless act of love. Because, as both were to think later, they just didn't seem to have much say in the matter.

If anyone had told her how exquisite the act of love could be after her unhappy experience of it she would not have believed them. Not even when she'd felt herself come alive in that particular way in his arms had she expected such rapture.

The way he touched her breasts and teased her nipples was divinely thrilling. The way his fingers sought her warm, silken, most erotic spots almost took her breath away. And because he was extra-gentle, not only in deference to her scrapes and bruises, his final claiming of her and their subsequent climax was so different from what she'd known it was the most amazing, joy-filled revelation.

Most of all, the knowledge that she'd

brought him equal pleasure was the cause of deep, deep satisfaction to her.

She was just about to tell him this when another huge crack tore the night air and the big old gum outside gave up its struggle to stay upright in the rain-sodden earth. With a crash, it cannoned down the hillside into the side of the shed.

They both moved convulsively, and Adam wrapped her securely in his arms. But although everything rattled, and a few things fell down, the shed withstood the impact.

'How do you feel?' he asked, after they'd waited with bated breath for more mayhem and none had come.

'Wonderful,' she said softly. 'I've never felt like that before. I can't believe it.' Little lines of laughter creased beside her eyes. 'I mean...' She hesitated and changed tack. 'How about you?'

An expression she couldn't identify crossed his eyes. But it was with his lips quirking that he said, 'Wonderful.' He sobered. 'Bridget—'

'No.' She put a finger to his lips. 'I don't want to dissect it. I just want to go on feeling wonderful.'

'Then let's see if we can get a bit of sleep. Comfortable?'

'Mmm...' she murmured drowsily.

They fell asleep in each other's arms, until dawn filtered through the grimy shed windows and they heard a helicopter's rotors beating overhead.

'Bridget—' Adam said, and stopped.

Here it comes, Bridget thought, the parting of the ways, the thing that had been on her mind ever since she'd woken in his arms and been flooded by the memory of their love-making.

She wore—they both wore—State Emergency Services orange coveralls. Hers were way too big for her—but far better to be hoisted into a helicopter in something that nearly smothered her rather than an old towel.

And they did have to be hoisted into the helicopter, because the ground was too soft and waterlogged for it to land. By contrast, however, it was a bright sunny day, the sky was a clear blue, and the drenching rain, howling winds and pyrotechnics of the night before were like a dream—of the nightmare variety.

They were still sitting in the helicopter. It had landed on a tarmac driveway, and they were waiting for an ambulance to transport Bridget to the Gold Coast Hospital for a check-up.

She'd strenuously objected to this, saying she was quite fine, but Adam had sided with the paramedic on the helicopter and she'd been effectively outvoted. She had been up-lifted by the news that the family in the car that had been washed away after hers had also been rescued.

'Bridget,' Adam said for the third time, and put his hand over hers. 'I'm not for you, and that's—'

'Not my fault but yours?' she murmured huskily, in a parody of the old 'it's not you, it's me' explanation.

He grimaced. 'Trite, but unfortunately true.' He paused. 'I'm lousy lover material, and I'd be terrible husband material.'

'Lousy lover material?' she whispered. 'I have to beg to differ.'

He lifted her hand and kissed her knuckles. 'You're sweet, but it was just one of those things.'

Bridget considered. It had seemed to her,

from the moment they'd woken to the sound of the rotors and both leapt out of bed, covering themselves with whatever they could find and racing out to flag down the helicopter, that they'd been tied to each other by an invisible string.

She reconsidered. As if they belonged to each other! But she'd certainly felt that, and could she have been so wrong?

She recalled the way he'd taken her back inside the shed and helped her into the voluminous coveralls, how they'd laughed a little together as she'd all but drowned in them. How he'd kissed her and told her it had to be an improvement on a horse rug.

Then they'd used a double harness to winch them up—he had seemed to know all about it, and also to know one of the crew—and she'd gone up in his arms.

He'd kissed her again when they were safely inside the helicopter, and she'd sat squashed up against him as it had risen and flown, squashed and in his arms, so her erratic heartbeats had normalised and she'd felt safe because they were *his* arms.

'Will you ever get over the woman who left you for your brother?'

He looked down at her, and there was something like compassion in his eyes that hurt her very much.

'I have got over her. It's my brother—but it's more than that. I'm far too old for you.' He stilled her sudden movement. 'In experience, in the kind of life I've lived, and in the far too many women I've loved. What you need is someone with no murky past, who can share an optimistic future with you.'

'And if I don't want—?'

'Bridget,' he cut in, and released her hand to wipe away the tears that sparkled on her lashes with his thumbs. 'If there's one thing you can take away with you, it's this: you were gorgeous in bed, and don't let any guy with an oversize ego tell you otherwise. You be selective, now, and make sure you give the men who are not good enough for *you* the flick.' He brushed away another tear and picked up her hand as his lips quirked. 'Incidentally, I'm one of those.'

'But I *loved* being in bed with you,' she whispered brokenly.

'There's a lot more to it than that.' He turned his head as an ambulance drove up and parked beside the helicopter. 'Your limo has arrived, Mrs Smith.' He raised her hand and kissed her knuckles again. 'So it's time to say goodbye. Take this with you.'

He rummaged in a seat pocket until he came up with a pencil and piece of paper, upon which he wrote a telephone number.

'If you need me, Bridget—' his eyes were completely serious now '—in case of any unplanned...*consequences*, this number will always get a message to me.'

Bridget took the piece of paper, but she couldn't see what was written on it. Her eyes were blurred with tears. Then it came to her that there were two ways she could do this. As a tearful wreck, or...

'And if you need me,' she said, dashing at her eyes as she raised her hand beneath his to kiss his knuckles, 'you know where to find me.'

They stared into each other's eyes until he said, very quietly, 'Go, Bridget.' His expression changed to harsh and controlled as a nerve flickered in his jaw, and he added, 'Before you live to regret it.'

Several hours later Adam Beaumont let himself into a hotel penthouse suite on the Gold

Coast, and strode into the bathroom to divest himself of the orange SES coveralls which had raised a few eyebrows in the hotel.

He took a brisk shower, dressed in jeans and a T-shirt, and padded through to the lounge.

But with his hand on the telephone he paused and thought about Bridget. Was she still undergoing examination for any unseen injuries? Or was she at home now?

It annoyed him momentarily to realise he couldn't picture her 'at home' because he had no idea where she lived. And it worried him obscurely to think of her at home, wherever that was, and alone. Not only after her amazing and dangerous adventure, but after their spontaneous lovemaking.

What had possessed him? he wondered rather grimly.

She couldn't have been less like the women he usually dated: soignée, sophisticated girls, well able to take care of themselves even when they discovered that he had no intention of marrying them. Not that he ever tried to hide it.

As to *why* he had no intention of marrying them, was it only a case of once bitten, twice shy? Once betrayed by a woman, in other

words? Well, there was also the disillusion-
ment of his parents' marriage at the back of
his mind, but even that, painful as it had been
as he grew up, did not equal his disbelief, the
raw hurt, the anger and cynicism, the desire
for revenge his now sister-in-law's defection
had provoked in him.

Strangely, though, he hadn't thought about
it in recent times—until a copper-headed girl
with green eyes had winkled it out of him
last night. And, yes, he thought harshly, it *did*
still hurt, so it was better packed away—along
with the whole thorny question of whether he
would ever trust a woman again.

But to get back to Bridget Smith—why *had*
he done it?

To comfort her? Yes. To prove to her that
her one previous experience had been no more
than a case of the wrong man? Yes.

Because he hadn't been able to help himself?

Well, yes, he conceded. And that had been
due to a combination of those green eyes, that
lovely, tender little body, her freshness, and
the simplicity and naturalness of her reactions.
Yes, all of that. Plus admiration—because she

had been brave and humorous, and those little touches of hauteur had secretly amused him. Even her outrageous lies on the subject of the non-existent Mr Smith had amused him.

It came to him from nowhere. Perhaps, if he was ever to take a—how to put it?—convenient wife, Bridget Smith was the kind of girl he needed?

He stared out at the view from the penthouse as he pictured it. Mrs Bridget Beaumont. Then a frown came to his eyes and reality kicked in. He was better off steering clear of *any* commitment to a woman. Far better off.

He shrugged and lifted the receiver to organise the retrieval of his Land Rover and the possessions in it. He was about to put the phone down when he thought that there was one thing he *could* do for Mrs Smith. He could at least facilitate the retrieval of *her* possessions, if not her car...

Bridget had had to get a locksmith to let her into her flat, although not much later—after she too had showered and changed out of her coveralls—a knock on her door had revealed yet another SES officer, bearing her overnight bag and her purse, both retrieved from her car.

She was immensely grateful, even though the news about her car was not good. It was going to have to be taken out of its final resting place piece by piece.

She closed the door on the officer and bore her purse to the dining room table as if it were precious booty. Once she'd checked everything and found it all there she sat back and looked around, feeling suddenly sandbagged as all the events of the previous twenty-four hours kicked in.

It was small, but comfortable, her flat: two bedrooms, open-plan lounge, dining room, kitchen and a pleasant veranda, on the second floor of a modern two-storeyed building in a quiet suburb not far from the beach.

Although she could have owned it—her father had divided his quite substantial estate between her and her mother—she'd decided to keep her nest egg from her father intact in case she ever really needed it.

She'd put quite some effort into decorating her flat, though. She'd used a cool green for the walls, with a white trim, and cool blues for the furnishings and rugs.

Cool was the way to go on the sub-tropical Gold Coast. But there were splashes of yellow and pink. Some fluffy yellow chrysanthemums in a pewter flask vase on her dining table—the vase had been a present from her mother, who lived in Indonesia these days. And some pink cushions on her settee, a fuchsia lampshade atop a pretty porcelain lamp.

There were also some of her own paintings on the walls. Paintings of flowers that flourished in the tropics—orchids, frangipani and hibiscus. Oddly enough, despite her assertion to Adam that she wasn't much good, she'd entered some of her paintings in a local art show, and the owner of an interior design firm that specialised in decorating motels, rental apartments and offices had bought all six. He'd also told her that he'd take as many more as she could paint, and no matter if she repeated herself.

So far she hadn't done any more. She wasn't quite sure how she felt about her work gracing the walls of impersonal motel bedrooms, rental apartments and offices. Did that make her a real artist, or something much more commercial?

But now, as she looked around, art—commercial or otherwise—couldn't have been further from her mind. Why wouldn't it be when she'd just gone through a unique experience and then had it torn away from her?

But as she thought of the man called Adam she had to acknowledge that from the moment he'd so reluctantly revealed his past history she'd known he was bitter about women. He'd told her himself he was a rolling stone, so it shouldn't have come as such a shock that he would walk away from her like that.

But it had, she conceded, and wiped away a ridiculous tear. Because their intimacy, for her, had been so perfect and such a revelation.

Had she unwittingly translated that into the belief that it must have been the same for him?

She grimaced sadly. That was exactly what she had done. But perhaps the bigger question now was—What was she left with?

A memory, to be pressed between the pages of a book until it dried and lost colour like a forgotten rose? A memory that evoked a bittersweet feeling in her breast that faded with time? Or a raging torrent of disbelief and anger that he could have made love to her so beautifully she suspected she would *never* forget it and then simply walked away?

CHAPTER THREE

'WHO'S *this*?' Bridget Tully-Smith was holding a newspaper and staring at a picture of a man on the front page. Her expression was completely bemused. 'I don't believe it...'

Julia Nixon, her colleague and friend, put her red high heels on the dull commercial-grade carpet of the busy TV newsroom and wheeled herself in her office chair from her cubicle to Bridget's cubicle, next door. She scanned the picture and caption, scanned Bridget in turn, then said carefully, 'What part of Adam Beaumont don't you believe?'

'But that can't be Adam *Beaumont*!'

'Oh, it is,' Julia murmured. 'In all his glory.' She frowned. 'Why can't it?'

Bridget put the paper down and turned to her friend. 'Because I met him.' She paused, and thought how inadequately that covered her encounter with this man roughly three weeks ago.

'He was—' She stopped, then went on. 'He wasn't part of the Beaumont empire! If anything he was very much a rolling-stone-that-gathers-no-moss type.'

'Well, he may be, but that doesn't stop him from being gorgeous or the real thing.' Julia stared at the picture with a pensive look in her grey eyes. 'Has he taken over from Henry Beaumont, his brother?'

Bridget perused the opening paragraph of the article accompanying the picture. 'There's a rumour, but that's all at this stage. How did you know?'

'High society is my department these days, darling,' Julia reminded her. 'You'd be amazed how many strange rumours I hear about the rich and famous when they party.' She smoothed her pale gilt hair and studied her long red nails with an expression Bridget couldn't identify.

Julia was in her thirties, an experienced journalist, with a penchant for red shoes, tailored grey suits and red nails to match her lips. She was extremely attractive, although she often exhibited a world-weary streak. She was unmarried but, talking of rumours, was said to have had—still had, for all Bridget knew—a series of high-profile lovers.

'For example,' Julia continued, 'Adam Beaumont is supposed to be estranged from the fabulous Beaumont mining family. He's certainly made his own fortune—out of construction rather than minerals.' Julia gestured. 'Further rumour has it that there's a blood feud between Adam and Henry Beaumont. And I wouldn't be surprised if Adam has finally found the lever to unseat Henry.'

Bridget's mouth fell open.

Julia raised a thinly arched eyebrow at her.

Bridget closed her mouth hastily. 'Nothing.'

'And I also wouldn't be surprised,' Julia went on, 'if he doesn't do as good if not a better job than his brother. I always had Adam Beaumont taped as a cool, tough customer who would be equally at home in a boardroom as a bedroom—he's as sexy as hell. Where did you meet him? It has to be him, I would say. You couldn't confuse that face easily.'

Bridget blinked at the picture in the paper and thought, No, you couldn't. 'Beside a swollen creek in a flash flood, trying to rescue a carload of people.'

Julia pursed her lips as she summed Bridget up from her short cap of coppery hair, her delicate features and her sparkling green eyes, her slender figure in a white-dotted voile blouse and khaki cargo pants to her amber suede pumps. 'You may have been lucky if you looked like a drowned rat.'

'Oh, I did.' Bridget paused with a grimace that turned to a frown. 'But—is he really a playboy?'

'He has escorted some of the loveliest, most exotic women in the land, but not one of them has been able to pin him down. Uh-oh.'

Julia wheeled herself back to her domain to answer her phone. And it occurred to Bridget as Julia did so that there was something in her colleague's demeanour that was a little puzzling. But she couldn't put her finger on it, so she turned her attention back to the picture in the paper.

Adam Beaumont was thirty-one, and good-looking. In the picture, he was wearing a suit and a tie, and he'd been captured on the move, with the front flap of his jacket flying open— not at all how she remembered him.

Despite his being soaked and unshaven that tempestuous night, and in jeans and boots, the two things she would always remember about him remained the same, however. It was the same tall, elegant physique beneath that beautiful suit, and the same haunting eyes—those often brooding or moody, sometimes mercilessly teasing, occasionally genuinely amused blue eyes.

It all came flooding back to her, as it had in the moments before she'd made the exclamation that had grabbed Julia's attention.

But for the time being she was to be denied the opportunity to think back to that memorable encounter with Adam Beaumont, whom she'd known only as Adam. It was an hour before the six o'clock news. The main bulletin of the day was to go to air, and the usual tension was rising in the newsroom.

She heard her name called from several directions, and she folded the newspaper with a sigh, then took a deep breath, grabbed her clipboard and leapt into the fray.

When she got home, she made herself a cup of tea and studied the newspaper again, at the same time asking herself what she knew about the Beaumonts.

What most people knew, she decided. That they were ultra-wealthy and ultra-exclusive. Adam and Henry's grandfather had started the dynasty as a mineral prospector, looking for copper but stumbling on nickel, and the rest, as they said, was history.

What she hadn't known was that the family was plagued by a feud, until Julia had mentioned it. The moment Julia had remarked on the possibility of Adam finding the lever to unseat his brother, Henry, it had taken her right back to the shed, the paraffin lamps and the storm, and that hard, closed expression on Adam's face. If she'd had any doubts that they were one and the same man, they'd been swept away.

Her next set of thoughts was that Adam Beaumont had probably gone out of his way not to reveal his identity—because, to put it bluntly, he was way out of her league.

Surely that was enough, on top of what he himself had said, to kill any lingering crazy longing stone-dead? she reflected—and wrapped her arms around herself in a protective little gesture.

Three weeks had seen her go through a maelstrom of emotional chaos. Her bruises and scrapes might have healed, but her mental turmoil had been considerable. And, as she'd postulated to herself the day she'd been both rescued and abandoned, she felt torn between a bittersweet *it was never meant to be* sensation and a tart resentment that left her feeling hot and cold. If he'd known he wasn't for her, why had he done it?

Of course she'd been more than happy to participate, but she hadn't had a cast-in-concrete conviction that she was a loner, had she? Moreover, shortly before it had happened, she had thought she was going to die. Had that accounted somewhat for her willingness in his arms?

But most of all, in these three weeks, she'd felt lonely and sad. She couldn't believe she could miss someone so much when she'd only known him so briefly, but she did.

She sniffed a couple of times, then told herself not to be weak and weepy, and turned her attention to the newspaper again.

She reread the article, but there was not a lot to be gleaned from it. It was simply speculation, really, to the effect that there could be moves afoot on the Beaumont board, plus some of the company's impressive mining achievements.

It also detailed some of Adam Beaumont's achievements outside the field of mining, and in their own way they were impressive. He was obviously a billionaire in his own right.

So what was it really about, this article? she wondered. It did detail that Adam was not a major shareholder in Beaumonts, whereas Henry was. And how did that line up with what she knew? The fact that Adam had sworn revenge against his brother and was looking for a lever to unseat him?

She shook her head, a little mystified. She stared at the photo of Adam Beaumont and suffered an intensely physical moment. It was as if she were right back in his arms, with that chiselled mouth resting on hers, his hands on her body thrilling and delighting her.

What a pity there was never any future for us, she thought, and blinked away a solitary tear. It was no good telling herself again not to be weak and weepy, because the fact remained there seemed to have been awoken within her a chilly, lonely little feeling she couldn't dispel, and—she stopped and frowned—a strange little echo she couldn't place.

Of course there was also the fear that she might have fallen pregnant continually at the back of her mind. A state which came under the heading of *consequences*, no doubt, she thought dryly. Statistically, she had decided—the time of the month, it only happening once—it was unlikely. Although she was realistic enough to know it was a statistic not to be relied upon.

But now there was a new feeling added to all her woes, she realised as she laid her head back and stared unseeingly across the room. And it centred around the fact that he'd allowed her to think he was ordinary when in fact he was a billionaire.

What difference does it make? she wondered.

She sat up suddenly. It makes me feel like a gold-digger, or as if that would have been his automatic assumption as soon as I found out! she answered herself.

And that outraged her, she found. Although a little niggling thought came to her—perhaps that was the way a lot of women reacted when they discovered who he was? Perhaps that had added to his cynicism about women?

She heaved a huge sigh and deliberately folded up the paper so his picture was inside, not visible. She forced herself to concentrate on her upcoming weekend. She, several others and a party of disabled children were spending the weekend on a farm. It was going to be arduous, and she would give it her all. She would not allow Adam Beaumont to intrude. And her period would come in the natural course of events when it was due, on Sunday.

But her period didn't come in the natural course of events, and by the following Sunday it still hadn't.

It would be fair to say that Bridget had held out until the last moment in her belief that her cycle had gone a bit haywire, but when a home pregnancy test proved positive she had to face the cold, hard truth.

She was pregnant after a one-night stand with a man she barely knew—a man who had told her unequivocally that he wasn't for her...

It was a shattering thought.

* * *

Two days after she had made the discovery there was a crisis in the newsroom.

Megan Winslow, who was doing the news on her own because Peter Haliday, her co-presenter, had the flu, fainted half an hour before air time.

Out of the chaos, Bridget was chosen to replace her. In the normal course of events it would most likely have been Julia chosen to do it, but it was her day off. There were several reasons to choose Bridget. She spoke well, with good modulation—she'd belonged to her university dramatic society—and she was familiar with the autocue as she'd occasionally filled in for the weather presenter.

'You've also proofed a lot of the stuff, so you're familiar with it. We can find you something more formal to wear,' Megan's producer said to her. 'Make-up!' he yelled.

It was a miracle Bridget managed to speak at all, considering the emotion-charged atmosphere of the newsroom. Even more than that, her own inner turmoil was mind-boggling. She hadn't been able to come to grips in any way with the fact that she was carrying Adam Beaumont's baby. If anyone should be fainting, she should...

But she actually got through reading the news with only a few stumbles. And she had no idea who would be in the unseen audience for that particular broadcast…

Adam Beaumont unlocked the door to his suite in the luxury Gold Coast hotel and threw the keycard onto the hall table. He walked through to the lounge, shrugging off his jacket and tie, and switched on one table lamp.

The view through the filmy curtains was fabulous. The long finger known as Surfers Paradise stretched before and below him like a fairyland of lights, bordered by a faint line of white breakers on the beach and the mid-night-blue of the Pacific Ocean, with a silver moon hanging in the sky.

He didn't give it more than a cursory glance as he got a beer from the bar and poured it into a frosted glass. He'd been overseas, and he was feeling jet-lagged and annoyed. One of his PAs had met him at the airport and given him a run-down of events that had occurred in his absence. One of them was a newspaper article described by his PA as a 'fishing expedition', to do with the board of directors at

Beaumonts and a carefully worded suggestion that there was some unrest on the board.

Where the hell had that come from? he'd asked, but had not received a satisfactory answer.

The Beaumont board, he thought, standing in the middle of the lounge, staring at nothing in particular. Ever since he could remember the family circumstances that had contributed to his distance from the board had galled him almost unbearably. And that had contributed, along with his faithless sister-in-law, to his determination to unseat his brother, Henry. But it so happened *he* hadn't done anything to create the rumours.

He put his beer on a side-table and looked around for the TV remote before he sank down into an armchair.

He was flicking through the channels when his finger was arrested, and he sat up with an unexpectedly indrawn breath as he stared at Bridget, reading the news.

She was wearing an elegant lime-green linen jacket, and her coppery hair was still short but obviously styled. Her eye make-up emphasised her green eyes, and her lips were painted a lustrous pink.

She looked, in two words, extremely attractive, he thought. But what the hell *was* this?

She paused, then launched into a piece she happened *not* to have proofed. Of all things, she stumbled on the Beaumont name. But she collected herself and went on to detail the fact that the rumours circulating were suggesting Henry Beaumont was about to be ousted from the Beaumont board by his brother, in a bitter power struggle.

It was the last item before a commercial break, and as had been agreed, to save viewers any confusion, Bridget said, 'I'm Bridget Tully-Smith, filling in for Megan Winslow tonight. Please stay with us for all the latest sporting news.'

Adam Beaumont stared at the television long after an advertisement had replaced Bridget's image. *Tully*-Smith, he thought incredulously. You didn't tell me *that*, Mrs Smith. His mind ranged back. Although you did mention your father was a journalist and was killed in an accident. So it's more than likely that your father was Graham Tully-Smith, famous investigative journalist—or notorious, if you happened to be on the receiving end of it.

And it just so happens, his thoughts ran on, you're the *only* person I've ever told about finding the right lever to unseat Henry. Is there a connection between these rumours that have sprung up out of nowhere and you, Bridget?

Bridget was exhausted when she got home.

Although she'd been heartily congratulated on how she'd handled things, doing the news had been a huge drain. And on top of that the Beaumont piece had deeply perturbed her.

It had taken her back again to that night, to the events in the shed, back to Adam Beaumont again, and to what he'd revealed to her. But not only that. Adam Beaumont was where an awful lot of inner turmoil resided for her now...

She had come straight home, only to find she didn't feel like going to bed.

Then she got a phone call from the TV station, from a receptionist named Sally whom she happened to know, with the news that Adam Beaumont would like to get in touch with her. Could they pass on her number?

She took an incredulous breath. 'What for?'

Sally replied, 'I don't know, Bridge. He didn't say. It wasn't actually him, anyway, it was his PA. Do you know him?'

'I—I've met him.'

'Well, maybe he wants to congratulate you on the news!'

'Uh…' Bridget thought swiftly. 'I really doubt it. I mean, I'd rather not.'

'That's OK. Although personally I would never say no to Adam Beaumont,' Sally remarked with a chuckle. 'I'll just say you're unavailable for personal calls. I've got it down to a fine art. Night, Bridget!'

Bridget put the phone down slowly, her eyes wide and a little stunned.

Why did he want to get in touch now? she wondered.

It must have something to do with the item about the Beaumont board she'd read on the news tonight. It couldn't be any other reason. But it had nothing to do with her. She hadn't even proofed the copy, let alone originated the item.

And there were several reasons why she didn't want to see him. Not yet, at least.

Sheer panic was one of them. How was she to tell him she was pregnant? How would he react?

She wasn't at all sure of *her* reaction, other than stunned disbelief, so...

She hardly slept at all that night, but it didn't occur to her that Adam Beaumont wouldn't take no for an answer.

The next morning was Saturday, so she was off work. It was the day after she'd read the news for Megan Winslow and refused to talk to Adam Beaumont.

So what she was doing was strolling down the beach at Surfers, breathing the fresh salty air, hoping it would help her to clear her mind.

The tide was in, tracing silvery patterns on the sand, and the gulls were in full working mode as they swooped over the shallows, fishing for little bait fish. It was a clear, sunny day. There were swimmers and an army of walkers.

There were also families on the beach, with children of all sizes and ages, and for the first time she stopped and sat on a dune to study them closely. The crawlers, the toddlers, the paddlers, as well as a couple of pregnant mothers nearby. It occurred to her that in the company of her friends' children she thought loosely about having a family herself, but with one striking ingredient missing—a suitable father—it had never been more than that. She'd never imagined herself pregnant.

She was conscious again of that little echo she'd detected within herself but been unable to explain, and for the first time since disbelief and panic had gripped her it came to her that there was another life in her care and under her guardianship. In the normal course of events she would grow like the two pregnant women on the beach, and then that new life would be born and would carry her imprint.

But what about her life in the meantime? she wondered.

Would a reluctant father, even if he gave her and more particularly the baby material support, be better than no father at all? Or would she chafe at the fact that she'd never been good enough for her baby's father? If she did, how would a child react to that? Was she better off being a single mother or not, in other words?

How did you bear the burden of single-motherhood amongst your friends and in your workplace, though? It probably wasn't so unusual, but she couldn't think of anyone she knew who was pregnant and without a partner.

It was at this point in her musings that someone tapped her on the shoulder.

'Yes?' she said, with extreme surprise. She didn't recognize the man and couldn't imagine what a formally dressed middle-aged man in a suit and tie was a: doing on the beach, and b: wanting with her.

'It is Miss Smith, isn't it?' he said. 'Miss Bridget Tully-Smith?'

Bridget opened her mouth to say yes, but then said instead, with a faint narrowing of her eyes, 'Who wants to know?'

'Mr Beaumont, Mr Adam Beaumont, would like a word with you, Miss Tully-Smith. I'm Peter Clarke. I work for him, and I just missed you coming out of your building a little while ago. I was trying to park. I was forced to follow you on foot, and—'

'Please tell Mr Beaumont I have nothing to

say to him at the moment,' Bridget interjected. 'And please tell him I don't appreciate being followed.'

She turned away and marched off, with her heart beating heavily.

She'd calmed down somewhat by the time she got home, and assured herself that if Adam Beaumont hadn't taken the hint before he would surely do so now.

Famous last thoughts...

She answered her doorbell late that afternoon to find him in person on her doorstep.

'You!' she gasped, and she tried to slam the door.

But he simply put his hands around her waist and picked her up, to deposit her inside the doorway.

'I'll scream!' she threatened, more out of frustration than fear.

'Scream away,' he invited. 'But I don't intend to close the door. I don't intend to deprive you of your liberty or harm you in any way, or stop you using your phone. I do intend to tell you this, though. The more you run away from me, Mrs Smith, the guiltier you look.'

This stopped Bridget dead.

She stared at him wide-eyed and with her mouth open. He was wearing the same suit he'd been photographed in, navy blue pin-stripe, with a matching waistcoat, but today it was a pale blue shirt he wore, with a burgundy tie.

That dark hair was the same, though. So were the austere lines of his face and mouth. It was the same pair of broad shoulders beneath the faultless tailoring, the same narrow waist and long legs. The same blue eyes—but today they were accusing and insolent...

'G-guilty?' she stammered. 'I haven't done anything!'

'How about failing to give me your full name, Bridget?'

'Th-that wasn't—I often don't use my full name,' she stammered. 'People always ask me if—if I'm—' She stopped and pleated her fingers together.

'If you're Graham Tully-Smith's daughter?' he finished for her. 'Graham Tully-Smith, investigative journalist extraordinaire. But there's more, isn't there? You work in the news department of a television station. You've even climbed the ladder a bit to read the news. All of which places you perfectly to pass on a juicy titbit you picked up one wet, stormy night in the Numinbah, doesn't it?'

'What do you mean?'

'Bridget,' he said deliberately, 'you're the only person I've ever told about my ambition to unseat my brother. Yet now it appears to be common knowledge.'

Bridget breathed confusedly. 'I didn't tell a soul,' she protested. 'There's no way I could have used it, anyway. I'm just a very junior gofer. That's all.'

He raised a cynical eyebrow at her. 'Is that how you came to be reading the news last night? Look—' he turned back to the open door '—we can continue this in public if you prefer, or…?'

'Oh. Close it,' Bridget said, distraught, and when he did, she went on, 'We had a crisis in the newsroom last night. Megan fainted. That's how I came to do it. And reading the news doesn't mean I had anything to do with *compiling* it!'

'Is that so?' He came back to stand in front of her, and she could see the suspicion in his eyes. 'Are you *sure* you didn't mention it, even in passing, to someone who may have been able to use it?'

'No. I mean, yes, I'm sure!' she cried, her eyes wide and shocked. 'Anyway, it was common knowledge before I found out who you were.' And she told him about Julia's re-action to the first newspaper article, although she didn't mention her name. 'She, my col-league, even used the same word you did—a lever,' she went on. 'But up until that moment I had no idea who you were.' She closed her eyes and swayed suddenly.

'Bridget?' he said, on a different note as he scanned her now ashen face. 'Are you all right?'

'I—I'm, yes,' she murmured, but sank down on the settee. She rubbed her face and com-manded herself to think clearly.

He hesitated, then sat down opposite her. 'Have you any idea how destabilising these kind of rumours can be? How shareholders can be affected—and share prices?' he added significantly.

'Of course.' She gestured. 'I mean, if I stop to think about it, of course. But I didn't. I haven't.' She grimaced as she thought that she'd had more than enough of an entirely different nature to think about recently. She lifted her lashes. 'Have *you* taken shareholders and share prices into consideration? You did tell me it was only a matter of time before you found the right lever to unseat your brother.'

He sat back. 'So I did. It so happens I haven't found it. It's a little complicated. But that's why I need to know exactly how these rumours started.'

He paused and studied her. She was wearing a white voile blouse and khaki cargo pants. Her feet were bare and her coppery hair was tousled. Her eyes were darker, and there was something about her that was different.

He removed his gaze from her as he pondered this, and looked around. It was pleasant, her flat, but very much exhibiting the simple pleasures of a home decorator. And rather reminiscent, for some curious reason, he thought suddenly, of the simple pleasure of making love to her.

In fact he had to confess that memories of that lovemaking had come back and taken him by surprise at some inappropriate moments...

Such as right now, he thought dryly. He could picture that slim, sleek little body moving in his arms, unfettered by any clothes. He could almost feel the lovely peachy curves of her hips beneath his hands, and he could feel his own body stirring in response. He suddenly realised she was staring at him with widening eyes, almost as if she could read his mind, and there was a tinge of colour mounting in her cheeks.

He looked away abruptly, but it crossed his mind to wonder about the power of the connection they'd made that night over four weeks ago. Of course circumstances had contributed to make it a unique occasion, but...

He deliberately stilled his thoughts there. It would never have worked then, and it certainly couldn't work now. If she had nothing to hide, why had she tried to evade him?

He sat forward. 'If I'm to get to the bottom of this, I need to know the absolute truth from you, Bridget,' he said. 'I'm prepared to wipe the slate clean if you had any involvement, *if* you agree to drop the matter.'

She took a deep breath. 'I had none,' she said simply.

He frowned. 'Why were you running away, then?'

Bridget stared at him. How could she tell

this harsh stranger who believed the worst of her that she was carrying his baby? It had been hard enough to contemplate telling the Adam she'd known and made love to, but now…

She tilted her chin. 'I was told to stay away, if you remember,' she said with quiet dignity.

He stared at her with several expressions chasing through his eyes—one of them a certain scepticism.

It was that scepticism that made her blood boil and her green eyes flash. 'But if you're imagining I spilt your secrets out of pique on that account, you're dead wrong, Adam Beaumont. Would you mind letting yourself out?' She came swiftly to her feet.

He stood up. And surprised her. 'Have you still got my phone number?'

She could only nod.

'If you have any other thoughts on the matter, give me a ring. In the meantime, I apologise if I misread you.'

'But you're not convinced?' she queried, barely audibly.

He shrugged and turned away, and she

watched him walk out of her flat and close the door behind him.

Bridget stared at the door, then dropped her head into her hands. It was all so surreal, and she couldn't believe it was happening to her. There seemed to be no link between the events of that stormy night and the present events. It was as if they'd happened to another person.

Come to that, it was as if there were two Adam Beaumonts. The man she'd felt so safe with, the man she'd loved making love to, and this formal stranger who'd just walked out on her.

Yet for a moment there it had been as if the mask had lifted a little. A moment when he'd concentrated on her figure and she would almost have sworn he'd been thinking about their time in each other's arms.

She rubbed her hands together as an extraordinarily clear mental picture came to her of his lean, strong hand on her breasts, her waist, her hips, of his mouth on hers and the way her curves had fitted into the hard planes of his body. It hadn't lasted, though, that moment when she'd thought he might have been thinking of them together that night. Perhaps she'd got it wrong?

As for his baby—she lifted her head and her eyes dilated—what was she going to do about that?

CHAPTER FOUR

ADAM BEAUMONT drove to his next appointment in a preoccupied frame of mind. There had been something about Bridget Tully-Smith he couldn't put his finger on—something that was puzzling him.

He'd been determined to see her because he'd been convinced she must be the source of the rumours sweeping the business world about the instability of the Beaumont board. And he'd been mentally kicking himself for allowing a slip of a girl to corner him into admitting what he had.

He hadn't thought he was going to die, he reflected with increasing irony, even if she *had*.

But if it hadn't been Bridget, who had it been?

* * *

He parked his BMW below a high-rise apartment building at Narrowneck and took the elevator to the penthouse, where his great-uncle Julius lived.

Now in his eighties, Julius Beaumont, his grandfather's younger brother, was confined to a wheelchair, but he still possessed a sharp brain and, at times, a cutting tongue.

The red velour drapes were pulled against the rainy dusk, and lamps gleamed on the polished surfaces of the heavy furniture. The building might be an ultra-modern tower, but Julius Beaumont was surrounded by antiques. Even his blue velvet smoking jacket belonged to another age.

And his chosen form of art—his passion in life, as it happened—adorned the walls: paintings of horses.

He inclined his white head as Adam came in, and by way of greeting said, 'Welcome, my boy, and what the hell is going on?'

Adam was under no illusions as to what he meant, and he replied accordingly, 'I don't know, Uncle Julius. How are you?'

'As well as can be expected,' Julius said testily. 'Help yourself, and pour me one at the same time.' He gestured towards the cocktail cabinet.

Adam poured two single malt Scotches into heavy crystal glasses and carried one over to his uncle. His own he took to an armchair.

'So you didn't decide to seize the bull by the horns and attempt to unseat Henry?'

'No.'

'Then who? And why?'

Adam sipped his Scotch. 'I'm somewhat at a loss. It could simply be shareholder uneasiness, but I've done nothing to promote that.'

'Hmm...' Julius swirled the amber liquid in his glass. 'You know, my boy, I've never meddled much in Beaumont affairs. It was Samuel's baby, not mine. But I do have a fairly significant holding. And I suppose I was loath to meddle in the natural order of things. Your father taking over from Sam, Henry taking over from Kevin when he died from all his excesses. Now I'm not so sure—did it ever occur to you that you were lucky, by the way?'

Adam smiled faintly. 'Frequently, but what particular aspect do you have in mind?'

'Both Kevin and Henry suffered from "rich man's son" syndrome, that's what,' Julius barked. 'Everything fell into their laps, and that doesn't build strong characters. But because they contrived to hold you away from Beaumonts, other than what you inherited from your mother, you went out and proved yourself in another direction. Did you the world of good.' Julius broke off and sighed. 'I'm getting on, and thinking of getting out.'

'Only out of Beaumonts, I hope you mean?' Adam murmured.

Julius thumped the padded arm of his wheelchair. 'The rest of it's not much fun, and when your time comes it comes.' He grimaced. 'But there's still something I want to accomplish. I want to see you settle down, Adam, my boy!'

'Thank you, but I *am* settled and—'

'No, you're not,' Julius contradicted him querulously. 'For one thing, you're still single.'

Adam shrugged. 'In the normal course of events I do have a few years up my sleeve.'

'In the normal course of events you wouldn't still be hankering for Marie-Claire, your brother's wife,' Julius shot at him.

Adam put his glass down. 'Uncle Julius,' he said coolly, 'don't.'

'You can't stop me!' Julius Beaumont had

the family blue eyes, old and rheumy now, but for a moment they flashed fire. 'I may never have married, but I know all about these heart-break girls: all eyes, all legs, take your breath away just to look at them. It's because of one of 'em I never did marry, if you must know.' He looked at Adam aggressively. 'Never told anyone that, and I don't expect you to repeat it.'

'I won't. She—broke your heart?' Adam hazarded.

'Damn near to it,' Julius agreed. 'And they may not make the best wives, necessarily. My nemesis married three times and never did get it right. Although in Marie-Claire's case she did marry Henry and give him two kids, whatever may—' He stopped rather abruptly.

Adam frowned, and waited as he wondered what Julius had been about to say. When his uncle didn't go on, he said briefly, 'That point has been made. And I'm getting a little tired of all this.' He picked up his glass to drain it.

'Then how about this?' Julius said sharply. 'If you show me you've consigned Marie-Claire and all that baggage to the past I'll hand over my proxies to you, so if there is uneasiness amongst the shareholders—and I wouldn't be surprised, because Henry's a fool—between us we would have the balance of power.'

Adam Beaumont found himself staring not at his great-uncle but at a magnificent grandfather clock that had fascinated him for almost as long as he could remember. The long gold pendulum swung backwards and forwards behind its glass door.

He forced his gaze back to Julius. 'Why?'

'I want to see Beaumonts back to its former glory for my brother Samuel's sake. And I don't want to see you drift down the years like I did, a confirmed bachelor until you find yourself in a wheelchair, with no one but paid employees to care about your welfare.'

'Uncle Julius,' Adam said firmly, 'that is a gross exaggeration.'

'Well, maybe,' Julius conceded. 'You've been very good to me, my boy, I must say.' He looked fretful. 'I've also got no sons to leave my estate to. So? What do you think?'

'How am I supposed to prove anything to you?' Adam asked carefully.

'One surefire way.' The old man smiled almost demonically. 'Take a wife!'

'I can't just go out and *take a wife.*'

'I wouldn't be at all surprised if you could take your pick of dozens of potential wives. But I'll tell you something: what you need to look for is a thoroughly *nice* girl. They're the ones who won't break your heart.'

'Even if I were to find "a thoroughly nice girl",' Adam said, then paused and narrowed his eyes as the phrase struck a chord in his mind. He couldn't place it. 'It could take time—and I'm not saying I will,' he added, with a slight barb in his voice.

'It's six months to the next shareholders meeting—unless they force one earlier.'

Adam stood up. 'Look, I'm sorry, I have to go. But I'll come and have dinner with you on Thursday.'

'But you'll think about it?' Julius stared up at him.

Adam paused. 'It's not that I'm not grateful, but if I do ever get Beaumonts I'd rather do it on my own. I mean that, Uncle Julius. I don't want to inherit it, in other words.'

Julius Beaumont watched Adam leave and shook his head. 'A dead ringer for his grandfather,' he muttered. 'As stubborn as a mule, yet what potential.'

But Adam didn't leave until he'd spoken to Mervyn, in the kitchen. Mervyn fulfilled the role of housekeeper and valet for Julius, and was a devoted employee as well as having had some medical training.

'How is he at the moment?' Adam helped himself to a slice of prosciutto that was destined to be part of the salad entrée for his uncle's dinner.

Mervyn removed the plate from his reach. 'We're a little up and down, Adam.' He often used the royal 'we' when discussing his employer. 'I had the doctor over yesterday, but he didn't think it would do any good to send him to hospital. He was of the opinion it would upset him more than help him. But I'm keeping a close watch.'

'Thank you,' Adam said. 'Actually, I can't thank you enough for the wonderful care you take of him. Oh, and I'll come for dinner on Thursday.'

'I know he'll look forward to that!'

Adam drove away even more preoccupied than he'd been before, and pondered his great-uncle Julius's health. Was he nearing the end? Was this concern he was showing an indication that he could feel the sands of time running out for him?

Funnily enough, he conceded, a chilly little image had come to mind, of himself drifting down the years and ending up alone with no sons to leave his estate to. But for the rest of it...take a wife and get Beaumonts...?

Not so simple, he thought, and recalled with a dry smile his uncle's remark about how lucky he'd been. Yes, of course he had been lucky in lots of respects, but growing up with an older brother who'd been the apple of his father's eye had not been easy. And had been made no easier when his grandfather had taken it upon himself to favour his grandson Adam over his grandson Henry. For some reason that had infuriated his father. Or perhaps there was no mystery to it, really.

There'd always been deep tensions between his father and his grandfather. But, whatever the ebbs and flows of disapproval between Samuel Beaumont and his son Kevin, there'd been nothing unseen about Kevin's preference for Henry. Not only that, they'd even looked alike—whereas Adam had favoured Samuel, and they'd had the same interests.

Nor had it all ended there. Grace Beaumont, Kevin's wife and the boys' mother, had bitterly resented Kevin's indifference to his second son and it had affected their marriage. They'd ended up virtual strangers.

If I did ever have sons, if I did ever have children, Adam Beaumont thought, I would never favour one above the other. Come to that, I'd *never* make them feel not wanted.

As for marriage—was it enough to marry even a thoroughly nice girl to ensure you didn't grow old and sad and lonely and ensure that you had heirs?

It was from that thought that he recalled where he'd heard the *thoroughly nice girl* phrase. The drenched Numinbah Valley via Bridget Tully-Smith, of course. The irony was that he'd even agreed with her at the time— but now…?

Bridget's mother rang her that night, and when she asked Bridget if anything was the matter it shot through Bridget's mind to tell her that she'd got herself pregnant by Adam Beaumont when she'd had no idea who he was. In the most amazing circumstances, granted, but that didn't absolve her from having acted incredibly foolishly. And, on top of all that, he now viewed her with extreme suspicion.

But common sense prevailed. The enormity of it all wouldn't fail to hit her mother and hit her hard. Probably enough to make her come racing home, which would be a pity. Her mother had been heartbroken at her father's death, and full of incredulity and anxiety when love had come to her again.

It had taken quite some power of persuasion on Bridget's part to get her mother to believe in this new love, and not to feel guilty about leaving her only child alone in Australia. Her mother's new husband, Richard Baxter, was an academic, and he'd accepted a year's fellowship at a Jakarta University.

He had a grown-up family of his own: a son who'd followed in his footsteps and a married daughter who lived in Perth. Even more importantly, he was the perfect partner for her mostly delightfully, sometimes maddeningly vague and unworldly mother. He really looked after her and cared for her, and they had lots in common.

The last thing she, Bridget, wanted to do was spoil that.

That was why she reassured her mother again that she was quite fine before she put the phone down. But, sitting alone in her flat later that evening, after the call, she knew that she wasn't fine. There were all sorts of moral and ethical dilemmas in front of her, not to mention getting her mind around a baby...

This is probably where you finally grow up, she told herself. First of all, you can't go on *not* believing it. And you probably shouldn't go on berating yourself. It's done now, and what is more important is that you don't make any more dodgy decisions...

She paused in her reflections as the word *dodgy* raised an echo in her mind—and that raised the other Adam in her mind's eye. The unshaven one, the man who'd saved her life, whose hands on her body had been such a revelation to her and brought her so much joy. How could she not want this baby? it suddenly occurred to her. Not to want it would be like negating something perfect...

She swallowed suddenly. But that perfection *had* been broken, she told herself. He didn't trust her, and there was no indication he could ever care for her...

She breathed in, distraught, and got up to get herself a glass of water.

If she decided to have this baby, she had to concede that she might have to do it on her own. Even if she did tell Adam Beaumont she was bearing his child, it would not necessarily lead to marriage—although she couldn't believe he would not offer some support. If she didn't tell him... Well, that had to be thought through thoroughly. It might, for example, suit her in some ways, but what about raising a fatherless child? What would that do to it?

She drifted over to the glass doors leading to the veranda and looked out at the night-time scene: the street lights, the garden inside the wall that protected it from the road, the cars, the wet slick on the road from an earlier shower. But she didn't see it at all as she grappled with what came to her suddenly as a crucial part of her problem. Whatever she did, she could not go on featuring as the villain of the piece.

She pulled a face at her turn of phrase, but it did clarify things for her. However she had this baby—whether there was a future or otherwise for her with Adam Beaumont—she had to clear herself of this stigma she'd acquired.

It was supremely important—because it affected her standing not only in his eyes but in her own.

How, though?

No answer came to her immediately, but in the middle of the night she sat up with a name on her lips—Julia. Why not start with her? She did seem to know something about the Beaumonts. Maybe Julia could at least point her in the right direction...

'Going away?' Julia asked on Monday morning, during their coffee break in the TV station's bright, bustling, impersonal cafeteria.

'Away?' Bridget looked at her, mystified.

Julia frowned. 'Don't you have three weeks' leave coming up tomorrow?'

Bridget could have kicked herself. How could she have forgotten? But, come to think of it, how fortuitous?

'Yes. No,' she said, and bit her lip. 'I mean, yes, I do, and, no, I'm not going away. I was—that is, I'm planning to potter.'

'Are you all right?' Julia queried.

'Fine,' Bridget lied. 'Julia, tell me more about the Beaumont brothers.'

'Why?'

'Just interested. It seems to be a fairly topical subject these days.'

Julia cut her blueberry muffin in half and buttered it before she responded. 'They were probably destined to feud from day one. Henry was always the apple of his father Kevin's eye, but the fact is neither Henry nor his father had the approval of Samuel Beaumont, Henry's grandfather. He was the founder of it all. And, while he didn't approve of his son or his eldest grandson, he *did* increasingly approve of Adam and see him as a more suitable heir. But Samuel died unexpectedly, and Adam got pushed more and more into the background. He was only twenty when Samuel died.'

'I...see,' Bridget said slowly. 'That wouldn't make for a happy family, precisely.'

Julia shrugged. 'No. Mind you, Adam branched out on his own and turned a medium-sized construction company into a billion-dollar enterprise. So he did justify his grandfather's approval, you could say.'

Bridget's lips parted. 'So why does he still—?' She stopped.

'Hanker for Beaumonts?' Julia supplied with a world-weary little smile. 'That's probably men for you. Power is important. He *is* a Beaumont. And Henry is seen by some as not doing a great job with the company. But there's also more, a woman—'

Julia broke off rather abruptly, and Bridget had it on the tip of her tongue to say *His brother's wife?* But she stopped herself on the thought that she had not yet revealed one word of what he'd said that night, despite what Adam Beaumont might like to think, and she wasn't about to start.

'Are the brothers alike?' she asked instead.

'On the surface, in some ways.' Julia paused thoughtfully. 'Henry's very good-looking, and quite charismatic, but…' She put her cappuccino down and patted her lips with a serviette. 'Why do *you* want to know all this, Bridge?' she asked rather intently.

Bridget shrugged. 'Just interested,' she repeated.

Julia Nixon looked at Bridget closely and noted the faint blue shadows beneath her eyes, testament to several sleepless nights. And she recalled Bridget's earlier confusion on the subject of her upcoming leave.

'Uh-oh,' she said. 'You fell for him, didn't you? Look, I'm probably wasting my time, but don't go there, sweetie. It's a no-go zone. Both of them are—as I know to my cost.'

Bridget blinked at her. 'What do you mean? How do you know to your cost? And what?'

Julia shrugged. 'I was Henry Beaumont's mistress.'

That evening Bridget, still reeling with shock at Julia's incredible revelations, dialled the number Adam Beaumont had given her with a shaking finger.

A disembodied male voice she didn't recognise said, 'Adam Beaumont's line.'

'Could I speak to Mr Beaumont, please?'

'I'll just check, ma'am. Who may I say is calling?'

'It's—it's—Mrs Smith from Numinbah.'

'Please hold on for a moment, Mrs—uh—Smith.'

Bridget held on until the voice came back.

'Adam can't leave his guests at the moment, Mrs Smith, but he'd be able to see you tomorrow morning at nine o'clock at the Marriott. Just ask for him by name. Thank you for your call.' The line went dead.

Bridget took the phone from her ear and stared at it in frustration. She'd been about to say that she didn't need to see Adam, she'd only like to talk to him, but the knowledge sank in that she might only ever be able to get a message to him—it was what he himself had said in the helicopter, although she'd had no idea why he would go to those lengths to protect his privacy at the time.

Now she did, and it ignited a spark of rebellion in her. How could he treat her like this? Even if he didn't know she was to be the mother of his child, it irked her tremendously.

It also prompted her to review her situation and make some plans. And she looked up pregnancy on the internet, so she would have a clearer idea of what she was in for.

Yes, she would see Adam Beaumont tomorrow—but only to clear her name…

She dressed with special care the next morning, in a straight green linen dress that matched her eyes, teamed with a cream jersey jacket and high heels. It was one of her more sophisticated outfits, suitable not only for the Marriott but for the Beaumonts. Then she had second thoughts. She looked as if she was going to a lunch, the races, or a job interview.

She took it all off and donned pressed jeans, a loose knit top the colour of raspberries and flat shoes. She cleaned off all the make-up she'd put on, but then her face looked pale and there were shadows under her eyes, so she started again using the barest minimum.

She'd washed her hair, so it was bouncy and shining with gold highlights. She regretted she'd not thought to get her fringe cut, but it was too late for that—and anyway, what did it matter?

And anyway, again, she would be running late if she wasn't careful, after all this dressing and undressing.

She threw her keys into her purse and raced downstairs to her new second-hand car.

She walked across the Marriott foyer at two minutes past nine. Two minutes later she was being ushered into Adam Beaumont's suite.

He was standing at the windows in the lounge, looking down on the view of Surfers sthe other day. She—she's authorised me to tell you all this: she was your brother Henry's mistress until recently, when he dropped her.' Bridget hesitated, then went on, 'Dropped her rather brutally, I gather. So she looked around for a way to get even with him.'

'Are you—?' Adam Beaumont frowned. 'Is this for real, Bridget?' he asked with supreme skepticism, and added dryly, 'You're going to have to do better than that if—'

'No, please listen to me,' Bridget broke in. 'She said that during their affair she formed the impression that your brother, Henry, had always had the fear that you were going to try and oust him. It seemed...' Bridget paused. 'It seemed to her that if she planted this rumour judiciously it might open up the way for you to take advantage of it, thereby gaining her some revenge. And even if you didn't manage to take advantage of it, it would make your brother's life quite complicated and difficult.'

She did not add that Julia had also given it as her considered opinion that neither Beaumont brother would ever get over Henry's wife.

He looked incredulous. 'Who is she? And has she no fear of any repercussions?'

'Julia Nixon.' Bridget waited until she saw the recognition come to him. He narrowed his eyes and his mouth hardened. Then she went on. 'She has no fears because she's advised your brother that if there *are* any repercussions she'll reveal that she was his mistress. She wasn't the first and most likely won't be the last, and she'll reveal that to the whole world, so his wife, and eventually his children, will have to know.' Bridget swayed a little where she stood. 'I know it sounds awful, but I do believe it's true and I do believe he hurt her really badly.'

'So…' Adam continued to gaze at her with a myriad of expressions chasing through his eyes.

'So it had nothing to do with me.' She swallowed several times. 'Nothing at all. It was pure coincidence that it came out not long after we—after you told me—after we—' Bridget broke off desperately, and then added in a smothered sort of rush, 'Oh, please, is there a bathroom handy? I feel very—sick.'

She *was* very sick, in the powder room of the penthouse suite. What was worse, she had no hope of hiding it from Adam Beaumont, because he was waiting for her outside the door. He took one look at her and led her to the main bedroom, where he sat her on the double bed and fetched a couple of flannels and a towel from the *en-suite* bathroom.

He started to wipe her face until she protested.

'You don't have to! Thanks, but I'm quite able to—'

'Bridget,' he broke in sternly. 'I've done much more than this to you before, so will you desist?'

She desisted in a feeble way, as she was swept by a memory of the things this man had done for her, and how he'd made her feel so safe. All the same, she had to protest. 'But—' she began.

He folded the second flannel and put it to her forehead. It was blessedly cool and soothing. 'Don't say anything,' he ordered. Then, a couple of minutes later, when her breathing had returned to normal, he added. 'Something you ate?'

'Probably.' But, since I have a cast-iron stomach, much more likely to be morning sickness, she thought.

He took the flannel away and frowned at her. 'Are you sure?'

She moved her shoulders slightly. 'Maybe nerves as well. I wasn't sure whether you would believe me, but it is all true.'

'I do believe it's quite possible, although I'll certainly check,' he said dryly. 'I don't know her well, but I would imagine Julia Nixon is cool and clever, and women scorned...' He shrugged and got to his feet. 'Which means I owe you an apology, Bridget. I hope you can see that it was the only thing that seemed to make sense.'

Bridget looked up at him. 'You really don't trust women, do you?' she said quietly.

He shoved his hands into his pockets and looked down at her meditatively. 'I don't trust anyone on face value.'

The thought ran through Bridget's mind *Then you're just as likely to believe this is not your baby—and that would be the final insult.*

'Oh, well.' She stood up. 'I'm sorry this happened.' She gestured to the flannels and the towel. 'I'll go now.'

He made an abrupt movement. 'Stay until you're sure you're fine.'

'No, thank you. I am sure.' She ran her fingers through her hair and straightened her raspberry top.

'I hope I haven't made you late for work, but I'm flat out at the moment.'

'No. I'm on holiday for a few weeks, and—' But she didn't have time to finish what she'd been going to say because his PA knocked on the door and called through that he was so sorry but Adam's next appointment had arrived.

Adam Beaumont swore softly beneath his breath, but Bridget smiled at him briefly and said, *'Adios!'*

And she left, gathering her purse on the way.

Fortunately, because she'd forgotten about it, she was at home when her friend Sandra from Numinbah arrived, with her baby, to spend the afternoon with her.

The baby girl, Daisy, was three months old now, and she slept through most of the afternoon. It was just before Sandra was due to leave that Daisy, in her cot, opened her eyes, saw Bridget looking down at her and smiled a blinding toothless smile as she wriggled joyfully.

Bridget couldn't resist it. She asked permission to pick Daisy up, and as the tiny girl snuggled into her shoulder a primitive age-old instinct overcame Bridget. For the first time the baby growing within her became a precious reality rather than a burden, and her options narrowed.

She thought of herself and Adam. Not the new, hard Adam, but the man she'd trusted and loved to be with. Joined for ever in a little person who was the result of their rapture and passion. Be it a boy or girl, there would be some of its father, some of the features she'd loved linked with hers. And, even more than that, it was a part of *her*, and as such it could only be a joy to her.

After Sandra had left, Bridget took a long, hard look at her whole life. It occurred to her that all the things she did well enough, if not brilliantly, while they might not fit her out to be a cutting-edge journalist might be useful as a mother. And she suddenly discerned that she'd lacked a goal in life—could fate have provided her with one in the form of this baby?

It was a discovery that caused the path that stretched before her to look a lot less rocky.

CHAPTER FIVE

A LESS rocky path didn't have any effect on morning sickness, however, as she discovered the next morning.

To complicate matters, she'd just started to feel nauseous, but thought she was holding it at bay, when her doorbell rang.

She hesitated, then went to answer it. It was Adam.

They simply stared at each other for a long moment, then he said, 'May I come in? I want to apologise. I've spoken to Julia Nixon and she's confirmed everything you told me.'

Bridget put a hand to her mouth, then took it away. 'I'm sorry, it's not very convenient.' She took a step backwards, then whirled on her heel and raced for the bathroom.

When she came back, she was pale but composed—and he was standing in the middle of her lounge with his hands shoved into his jeans pockets and a frown in his eyes.

He took a long moment to scan her from head to toe. She wore a brown summery dress patterned with white dots, in a clinging crêpe material. It had a scooped neckline and came to just above her knees. With it she wore brown backless moccasins with white laces. Her face had obviously just been washed; it was free of any make-up and there were damp strands in her fringe. She looked younger than her years, though, and somehow vulnerable.

'Bridget,' he said abruptly, 'is this morning sickness?'

She looked away as she wondered how to deny it.

'Two mornings in a row?' he said, as he scanned her pale face.

Her shoulders slumped. 'Yes. But I wasn't sure how to tell you, or even if I would.'

'You weren't going to tell me?'

She winced at the way he said it, then soldiered on. 'There didn't seem to be much point, since there's no future for us. Besides which I wouldn't be at all surprised if you don't believe it's yours. But I absolutely refuse to go through any DNA testing.' Her eyes suddenly glinted green fire at him. 'I know whose baby this is, and that's enough for me.'

A long, fraught pause developed as he digested this. She couldn't read his expression, but she saw that nerve flickering in his jaw and knew what it boded—Adam Beaumont at his most controlled and harsh.

'You're not its only parent,' he said.

She shrugged. 'I may not be, but I'm its crucial parent at the moment, and to my mind that gives me the right to call the shots.'

As she said it tears ran down her cheeks, and she licked their saltiness from her lips and wondered why she should be crying when she felt so angry. It came to her that all her anger and hurt had boiled over at last—anger that he could have loved her and walked away from her; hurt that he could have believed she would spread rumours about him because it was in her blood, inherited from her father, or because she was silly and thoughtless.

He had also automatically assumed she would pursue him if she ever discovered he was who he was, so he'd let her go on thinking he was just a run-of-the-mill guy who was wary of any attachment...

She licked her lips and dashed at her eyes.

'You see, Adam Beaumont, not only am I its crucial parent, but I know you don't want me. You don't trust me, you couldn't have made it clearer. So I've made my own plans. You can stay and listen to them or you can walk away again, but this baby is *my* affair and will be quite safe with me.'

'Why?'

The one word seemed to echo around the room.

'What do you mean?' she asked at last.

'Why do you even want it if you hold such a list of grievances against me?'

Bridget put her hands on her belly. 'Because it's part of me,' she said, quietly but quite definitely. 'And because it's part of you— the part that made me feel as I'd never felt before. I know now that was not the whole you and never could be, but on that one night it was special to me,' she said with painful honesty.

'Sit down,' he said, and gestured to the settee.

'Look, this is my apartment,' she flashed back. 'I can invite you to sit down *if* I want to, but you can't order me around!'

He grimaced. 'Would it be possible for

both of us to sit down and discuss this rationally?'

She hesitated.

'Perhaps we could even have a cup of coffee—?'

'Don't mention coffee,' Bridget broke in with a shudder. 'It's what set me off yesterday morning.'

'Tea, then?'

'Black tea would be nice,' she said slowly, and moved towards the kitchen.

'I'd offer to make it, but I wouldn't want to upset you.'

'Sit down.' Bridget pointed to the dining table.

'And shut up?' he offered softly.

She had to smile—the most fleeting of smiles, gone almost before it was formed, but somehow the tension between them was reduced.

'So tell me about these plans,' he said when she'd made the tea.

'I thought I'd keep working for a while,' she said. 'But it's been dawning on me slowly that I may have taken up journalism as a tribute to my father's memory rather than because it was something I was passionate about. So to leave it is not going to be devastating.'

She nibbled a dry biscuit and went on. 'Naturally I would like to have a career, but until one recommends itself to me, and while I'm pregnant and then looking after a new baby, I intend to start painting again.'

She pointed to one of her pictures on the wall, a claret-red cluster of frangipani blooms on a heritage-green background, and told him about the offer that had been made to her. 'I think it would be a rather perfect occupation for the time being—and I'm actually looking forward to it. Financially I'm fairly secure in any event, until the baby is about two. Then I will need to earn somehow or other.'

Adam Beaumont sipped his tea. 'I take it you've thought all this out in the context of me not knowing about the baby?'

'Well, yes,' she conceded.

'And now?'

Their gazes clashed.

'I...' Bridget stopped and started again. 'I don't really know what to think now. I mean—do you *want* to have anything to do with it?' she asked in a strained voice.

He closed his eyes briefly, in obvious disbelief. 'Bridget, I may have let you down and not trusted you, but do you honestly believe I'd be content to let a child of mine go through life never knowing me?'

'But those are the things I *don't* know about you,' she said hoarsely. 'And I don't know how it would work—'

He interrupted her in a hard voice. 'Then I'll tell you about me. I grew up virtually without a father. He hated me because I reminded him of his own father, who was a cruel man. But Henry could do no wrong. From my earliest memories nothing I ever did was good enough for my father. He and my mother fought over it. They didn't speak to each other for years. I left home when I was sixteen because I didn't think I was wanted and I never went back. And the bottom line to it all is this,' he went on. 'No, I wasn't planning to have children, but now it's happened, and if you think I will allow any child of mine to suffer the lack of a proper father, you're wrong, Bridget.'

Bridget closed her mouth. It had fallen open not only at what he'd revealed but at the bitter intensity he'd shown.

And although his expression was wiped clean and unreadable as soon as he'd finished speaking, he got up and walked over to the window, and she could see the tension in the lines of his back as he stared out at the street.

She was not to know that Adam Beaumont had surprised himself with the depth of feeling this news had provoked in him. Nor was she to know that the more he thought about it, the more he was struck by the irony of the situation. His uncle causing him to look at his life and his future so recently was one of those ironies.

A certain rumour associated with his sister-in-law, although he didn't know if it was true, was another. But his mouth hardened at the thought of it, and the bittersweet revenge he could exact with this news...

There was also, though, the fact that even if he was suspicious of or impatient with this baby's mother, he still felt protective towards her.

In fact, he discovered, not only could he offer his own child a proper father, and that was paramount, but the more he thought about it he also had the belief that there was only one solution, and it was growing in him by the moment...

'I—I'm sorry,' she said, barely audibly. 'I had heard… Julia did mention the divisions in your family, but I didn't realize—'

He turned back to her abruptly. 'It's over and done with now.'

'But what are we going to do?' she queried. 'Of course I wouldn't stop you from having access to it.'

Access… The word seemed to rebound on Adam, and he pictured it: a child with two homes, a child never quite sure where its allegiance should lie, a child possibly with a stepfather whose influence he, its real father, would have no control over.

'I don't want access when and where it suits you, Bridget,' he said harshly. 'There's only one thing to do. We need to get married.'

It took a moment or two for this to get through to Bridget, and when it did she stared at him incredulously. 'You can't be serious!'

'I am.'

'But we don't love each other. We hardly know each other! I don't even think we *like* each other now, and you certainly don't trust me—how can we?'

'Bridget.' He came back to the table and

towered over her. 'You can't have it both ways.'

She looked up at him uncomprehendingly. 'I don't know what you mean.'

'You've laid a few serious charges at my door, but I'm offering to redress the let-downs and the hurt to the best of my ability. Don't you believe a child deserves both its parents?'

She moistened her lips. 'Yes, of course—although it didn't seem to work very well for your parents, and that's what we would have to be afraid of—marrying then falling out badly,' she couldn't help but add. And then she thought of more objections. 'How come you're not accusing me of all sorts of crimes?' She waved a hand. 'Like trying to trap you or foist someone else's baby on you?'

'I was the one,' he said slowly, 'who initiated what happened that night. You were the one who got yourself clobbered by a falling branch. I really don't think you were in a fit state to set about trapping me.'

'I have to agree,' Bridget said dryly. 'But, to be scrupulously honest, I didn't do anything to stop you either.'

He grimaced. 'Also, I was wrong about you

and those bloody rumours. That's why I'm here. And I can't mistake your determination to go it alone. None of it fits in with a girl on the make. The other thing is, you're a terrible liar.'

She moved convulsively but he took her hand. 'No, just listen. I mean that as a compliment—not that you lie really frequently or well. As in the case of Mr Smith.'

Bridget subsided somewhat.

'And—' he studied her narrowly '—you're deadly serious now, aren't you, Bridget?' He waited.

She nodded at last. 'But I'm not going to do anything I may later regret,' she murmured. 'And, forgive me—I do appreciate your feelings now I know them—but marrying you could fall into that category. We just—we just don't know each other.'

A fleeting look that was so grim touched his eyes as their gazes locked. She shivered involuntarily, but she didn't look away.

His lips twisted. 'I should have known there was a touch of steel in you.'

Bridget raised her eyebrows.

'Yes,' he went on. 'A lot of girls would have been content to sit and wring their hands rather than put themselves at risk, struggling down a flooded creek in a God-almighty storm to save some children.' He shrugged. 'Think of this, though. *This* child is going to be with us for the rest of our lives. However it happened, we've forged that link and it can't be broken. But—and forgive me for saying this—' a wry little gleam lit his eyes '—the *way* it happened was quite amazing, I thought.'

Bridget's gaze fell before his at last, and a little pulse started to beat at the base of her throat. At the same time some pink coursed into her cheeks. If all that wasn't enough of a give-away of the power of her memories of that night in his arms, a little tremor ran through her.

He said nothing, but when she looked up she knew her disarray had been noted and filed away, probably for future reference.

She licked her lips. 'Are you not even a little surprised, let alone reeling from shock like I was?' she queried huskily.

He let her hand go, but pushed her hair out of her eyes with one long finger as a smile twisted his lips. 'Of course. But then nothing we do is simple and straightforward. It's always been one thing out of the blue after another.'

She had to concede this with a slight smile of her own. It faded as a sudden thought came to her. 'Does this have anything to do with your brother's wife?'

He frowned. 'What do you mean?'

Bridget thought back to Julia's other revelation—her considered opinion that neither Adam nor Henry Beaumont would ever get Henry's wife out of their system.

She said slowly, 'If you can't have her you'll have to make do with second best, and *this* second best—' she patted her flat stomach '—has the advantage of coming as a package deal?'

'On the contrary,' he said, looking very directly at her. 'This has nothing whatsoever to do with my brother's wife. You never did, Bridget.'

'I wish I could believe you,' she murmured.

'Why don't you let me show you?'

She blinked at him and said a little warily, 'H-how?'

'Well, first things first. Come and see my place. It's about an hour's flight away.'

She lifted her eyebrows at him. 'Fly? Just like that?'

'I have my own helicopter.'

He not only had his own helicopter, he piloted it himself. And the speed with which he organised the day almost took Bridget's breath away.

He called his bright young assistant, Trent, and they went through all his appointments for the day and rescheduled them.

'Uh, by the way,' Adam added, when his diary had been sorted out, 'I forgot to tell you, but I'm having dinner with my great-uncle Julius—let me see—tomorrow night. Ring up his housekeeper and tell him I'm bringing a guest. Thanks, Trent.' He clicked off his phone and turned to her. 'Ready, Bridget?'

She was only able to nod dazedly.

He piloted her towards his property in the Rathdowney Beaudesert area, over the Great Dividing Range from the Gold Coast. They flew over rugged country and he actually circled the creek they'd followed that tempestuous night, and the grassy plateau that had been their saving.

The shed looked smaller than she remembered. The tree had been removed, but the scar where it had uprooted itself on the hillside was still a raw gash.

'I never did get around to replacing those pyjamas,' she said ruefully into her mike, above the noise of the rotors.

'Don't worry. I compensated the owners. They're a youngish couple, and they do use the shed on weekends while they build their house. See the foundations there?'

She nodded as she followed the line of his finger, then was struck by an unanswered question she had.

'What *were* you doing driving around the Numinbah Valley in that elderly Land Rover that night? Especially if you can fly in this?'

He patted the control panel. 'This bird had mechanical problems, but I needed to get back to the Coast so I took one of the property vehicles and took a back road. It's hard to imagine being worse off that night, but if I'd flown into those storms I might have been.'

Bridget shivered.

* * *

Half an hour later he landed the helicopter on a concrete pad and said, 'Welcome to Mount Grace, Mrs Smith.'

Bridget stared around with parted lips. 'Oh,' she said. 'Thank you. It's—so beautiful.'

She was even more impressed after a guided tour.

Being over the Range was like being in a different world from the sub-tropical coastal plain. Here there were great golden, grassy paddocks, and there was little humidity in the air. It was still hot, but it was a different kind of heat, and you could imagine cold, frosty winters and roaring fires.

Nor did the vegetation resemble the tropical profusion of the Coast. There wasn't a palm tree in sight, but the gardens were magnificent all the same—even if not tropical—and the homestead, sheltered in the lee of a wooded hill, was a delight.

White walls, steep thatched roofs, French doors leading onto a paved terrace, and an unusual design of circular rooms. And the whole length of the terrace was dotted with terracotta tubs holding every coloured flowering bougainvillaea you could imagine.

The occupants of the great grassy paddocks were mostly horses, mares and foals, although deep rich red cattle were to be seen too.

'So—you breed horses?' she turned to ask Adam.

'It's my hobby. My uncle Julius—he's my great-uncle, actually—is my partner. He lives for horses. It's his greatest ambition to breed a Melbourne Cup winner. He used to go down for the race every year. He's not well enough these days, but he's a mine of information on the Cup.'

Bridget smiled to herself, but didn't explain why. Instead she turned back to the house. 'It's—it's very unusual.'

'It's a South African design. Thatched roofs and rondavels—round rooms—are traditional and common over there. My mother was South African. Her name was Grace.'

'So she's no longer alive?' Bridget queried.

'No. She and my father were killed in a car accident.' He paused, then decided not to tell Bridget that his father had been drunk at the time. 'Come inside and have a look, then we'll have lunch. Do you feel up to lunch?'

'I feel...' Bridget drew some deep breaths of the clear air '...dangerously hungry, as it happens. I would kill for some lunch, in other words.'

He grinned.

Mount Grace homestead was vast and cool. There were no ceilings to hide the soaring thatch roof, the floors were polished wood, and there were stone fireplaces in all the rooms.

The main lounge-dining area was exquisitely furnished. Some of the furniture was in woods she didn't recognise, and looked very old. There was a zebra skin on one wall, and a Zulu shield that reminded her of the movie of the same name.

'All in all,' she said, breaking her rather awestruck silence, 'there's one phrase that springs to my mind—out of Africa.'

'Yes—ah, there you are.' Adam turned at a sound behind them. 'Bridget, this is Fay Mortimer—housekeeper extraordinaire.'

'No such thing,' the middle-aged woman who stood before them replied. 'I'm sorry I wasn't here to meet you, but I had my hands full. How do you do, Bridget?'

They shook hands.

Fay Mortimer might be middle-aged, but she was slim and trendy-looking, with a shining bob of grey-streaked brown hair.

'Hands full?' Adam queried.

'I'm babysitting my granddaughter today. She's only three months,' she said to Bridget. 'But I have got lunch ready, and I thought it might be nice for you to eat on the terrace?' She raised an eyebrow at Adam.

'Sounds good to me. We're ready when you are. Bridget is actually starving.'

'Right-oh! You sit down. I'll bring it out.'

Lunch was delicious: a light consommé followed by a Caesar salad laden with smoked salmon, anchovies, and crispy bacon pieces. There were warm rolls to go with it, and it was followed by a cheese platter, biscuits and fruit.

As they ate, and Bridget sipped iced water while he had a beer, he told her about the stud and the stallions he had. He told her that Fay Mortimer's son-in-law was stud master, and lived there with her daughter—the mother of the three-month-old baby she'd been looking after. He also told her that they all lived in apparent harmony, although in separate cottages on the property.

It was utterly peaceful as they ate, with bees humming through the flowerbeds and dragonflies hovering, their transparent wings catching the sunlight. And the view was spread before them like a lovely sunlit tapestry under a blue, blue sky.

But when she'd finished Bridget laid down her linen napkin and said, 'I can't just walk into all this.'

Adam plucked a grape from the cheese platter and toyed with it in his long fingers. 'Why not?'

She hesitated, then swept her hair out of her eyes and took a sip of water. 'All this—it doesn't seem right.'

He ate the grape and plucked another, but it must have had an imperfection because after he'd studied it he tossed it into the shrubbery. 'I don't really understand what "all this" has to do with it. Are you trying to say if I'd been a wood-chopper at a country show you'd have married me?'

'That's ridiculous,' Bridget replied coldly.

'Why?' He stared at her derisively.

'Because—well, apart from anything else it is *obviously* not a good idea to marry anyone you don't really know!' she said through her teeth, and felt so frustrated she picked up the last few grapes on the stem and threw the lot into the shrubbery.

'Temper, temper,' he admonished softly.

'You started it!'

'Well, before we denude the table, may I point out that we *do* know each other pretty well in one way—the way they euphemistically refer to as the *biblical* way.'

Bridget had gone from angry to feeling slightly embarrassed at her rather childish display, but this taunt brought a tide of bright scarlet to her cheeks. She said, with as much dignity as she could muster, 'It's not the only way you need to know someone.'

'No, but it helps greatly if all is well in that direction,' he said wryly.

It was Bridget's turn to stare at him, and then to draw a deep breath and say, 'I appreciate your offer, but I'm of a mind to do this on my own.'

He swore under his breath.

'As for all this,' she continued, with a sweep of her hand, 'it's a bit like a carrot being dangled in front of me.'

'I wouldn't put it like that.' He eyed her narrowly. 'But I would see it as an apt setting for a girl who's told me she loves horses, gardening, painting. It could be a landscape painter or a gardener's dream—and there's a grand piano in the music room we didn't get to see, as well as a harp, come to think of it.'

Bridget was silent.

'You don't think that would make life enjoyable for you?' he queried.

She looked around, and had to smile involuntarily as a mare and a frisky young foal wandered up to the fence on the other side of the garden. But she sighed as she said, 'You don't understand, do you? Or—and this could be another problem—you're so used to getting your own way you don't want to understand how I feel.'

'I have to admit I would have understood better if you'd jumped at the chance—not so much of marrying me but of getting my money.'

'Ah. Well, I'm glad I surprised you.' Her words were accompanied by a lethal little look.

It was his turn to stay silent. Then he pushed his chair back and changed the subject completely. 'Come and say hello.' He indicated the foal.

She got up and followed him to the fence. On the way she pulled up a dandelion, which she offered to the foal. The dark bay colt sniffed it, lipped it, then chomped it greedily.

She laughed and rubbed his nose.

Adam Beaumont smiled and turned to lean back against the fence. He said quietly, 'I've had cause to think I should rewrite my life recently.'

Bridget turned to him in some surprise. 'You have?'

He nodded and stretched his arms along the fence. And then he told her something of his last encounter with his great-uncle Julius.

'I don't want his proxies,' he said. 'If I do ever get to chair the board of Beaumonts I want to do it on my own. I don't want anyone ever to be able to say I rode there on my uncle's coattails. But for the rest—'

he shrugged '—it is time to bury the past. Including Marie-Claire.'

Marie-Claire, Bridget thought. Just her name says it all...

'And I can't get this bleak little image of ending up on my own like Julius out of my mind,' he said with obvious frustration. He looked fleetingly wry. 'Perhaps that's why we need each other.'

Bridget opened her mouth, but he waved her to silence.

'I played God that night in the shed,' he said. 'I should have known better. I did. But it was a page we wrote together, Bridget. If it's brought more than you bargained for, the same goes for me. Even so, you obviously don't feel like tearing it up and throwing it away, and neither do I.' He paused. 'Despite everything, there's a *right* feeling to it.'

Bridget stared at him with her lips parted.

He had been looking into the blue yonder over her head, but now brought his gaze down to her. 'I know it's not a declaration of undying love, but that's the truth. And, contrary to what you said earlier this morning, I *do* like you.' His lips twisted. 'A lot.'

He reached out and brushed her hair out of

her eyes. 'I don't like to think of you alone, and even if you have decided it's your brave new world—and I'm sure it will be that from time to time—it doesn't need to be.'

CHAPTER SIX

IT WAS the sound of a car driving away that broke the spell for Bridget—that long, long moment when she was mesmerised by what he'd said, what he'd admitted, and the impact it had had on her.

'Who…?' she whispered.

He looked across at the departing plume of dust on the driveway behind the house. 'Fay. If we have no dinner guests she takes the afternoon off.'

'Oh.'

He looked at her wryly.

'I'm just a little speechless,' she confessed.

'You've offered me advice yourself,' he reminded her. 'To move on,' he elucidated.

'I know, but I didn't expect to—' She couldn't go on.

'To feature so prominently in it?' he suggested, humour glinting in his eyes.

'No.' She took a shaky little breath. 'But when you put it like that, it's terribly tempting. It sounds like a partnership. It sounds—sensible. But that's what it is, isn't it?'

He frowned. 'What do you mean?'

'It's...' She sought for the right words. 'It's a marriage of convenience, really.'

He didn't speak for a long time, then said, 'But that seems to recommend itself to you?'

She shrugged.

'Bridget,' he said slowly, 'I made some of the worst decisions of my life in a rush of—of passion, I suppose you could say. But respect, affection, and something to build on like a child, our child, recommends itself to *me*, yes.'

'I—I still need to think about it,' she murmured in some confusion—because his words, while so sane, seemed to strike a little chill through her. 'You must see that—well, it's the last thing I expected, and—'

'No, I don't think you need to think about it,' he contradicted. 'There can't be any reason why it isn't the best solution. You've told me your life—careerwise, anyway—is probably due for an overhaul. Is there *anyone* in your life it could make the slightest difference to?'

'No,' she denied. 'There's no one. Apart from my mother, and whatever I do is going to take her by surprise.'

'Then is there any reason to deny this baby both its parents in a secure home? Is there any reason not to put its welfare before everything else?'

Bridget turned away suddenly as his gaze bored into her. Was she thinking only of herself now? Was the fact that Adam had so much to offer—billionaire status, in other words—irrelevant really? She'd accused him of dangling a carrot before her, but perhaps that was immaterial. So what was behind her reluctance? Her own feelings?

Or a secret, inner suspicion that she was far better off without an Adam Beaumont who didn't really love her, even though he respected and felt some affection for her?

How selfish was that, though?

'Bridget?'

She turned back at last. 'I—maybe you're right.'

'Should we do it, then?'

Bridget discovered that she couldn't speak, because a fine trembling had started within her and had spread so that she was shaking from head to toe, shaking and feeling quite incapable of coherence.

She was unaware that she was also paper-pale and her eyes were as dark as emeralds.

Adam Beaumont cursed beneath his breath as he read accurately the enormous strain she'd been under, was still under, and did the only thing he could. He put his arms around her.

She didn't resist, but she didn't respond either—not for an age, at least. But gradually his warmth and the solid, secure feel of his arms got through to her, and she laid her cheek on his shoulder.

'I'm sorry,' he said, barely audibly. 'But you will be safe now.'

Bridget rested against him as all sorts of thoughts ran through her mind. One seemed to stand out. It was his child she was carrying and he did want it. Surely she owed that to the new life within her?

Her thoughts ran on. Did that not transcend any doubts she had that he might never have her in his heart the way he did the mysterious Marie-Claire?

Here her thoughts performed a little jig, so much so that she suddenly found herself wishing she'd never heard that name—because it seemed to embody for her an allure and a magnetism no man could resist.

I'll have to get over that, she cautioned herself, if I do this.

'Bridget?' He slipped his fingers beneath her chin and tilted it so he could see into her eyes.

Her lips parted. 'All right. Yes, I will marry you. Thank you,' she whispered.

He hesitated, as if about to say something, then changed his mind and lowered his mouth to hers.

She stood quite still in his arms, waiting for the magic to start to race through her, but nothing happened.

He lifted his head. 'Still worried, Mrs Smith?' he queried.

'I think I must be.'

He looked pensive. 'You don't suppose I need to conjure up a wild storm and an old shed?'

Bridget's eyes widened.

He traced the outline of her mouth. 'You may not realise this, and I certainly have not given you cause to, but I've thought of us together, when it was the last thing I should have been thinking of.'

'You have?' She blinked at him.

'Yes. For instance, I happened to be in a business meeting and I found myself doodling something most—unusual for the kind of meeting it was—a blue teddy bear, of all things. And that led to all sorts of inappropriate thoughts about you—and us. It wasn't my best meeting.'

Bridget smiled faintly and leant against him. 'That's nice, though. I don't mind being associated with blue teddy bears.'

His lips twisted and his hands moved on her hips. 'It was what was under them that caused me more embarrassment.'

She looked into his eyes. 'Really?'

'Oh, yes.'

She studied the rueful look in his blue eyes, the darkness of his wind-ruffled hair, and a little inner tremor ran through her that was quite different from the panicky tremors she'd experienced before. Not, she found herself thinking, that he looked as he had that night in the shed. He was clean-shaven now, and although he'd discarded his tie, and his shirt was open at the throat, and he'd rolled up his sleeves, he was still Adam Beaumont—not just a man called Adam…

Or was he?

Had the way he'd recalled memories of that night brought the other Adam to mind? Something had. Something about him was awakening her senses—senses that she had begun to think had been bludgeoned to death under the weight of all the trauma. Something was causing her fingertips to tingle with the longing to be able to touch him and her body to thrill at his closeness.

Perhaps it was something quite simple— he'd bewitched her almost from the first moment.

She took a breath that was a little sigh of relief. 'You're back,' she murmured.

'Back?' he queried, barely audibly, his breath stirring the fringe on her forehead, a question in his eyes.

'I—I've thought there were two of you. The man in the shed and Adam Beaumont. Sometimes,' she explained, 'I had these wonderful memories; at other times they were so sad because you were so different.'

'I'm sorry.' He kissed her forehead and then, after they'd stared deeply into each other's eyes, he sought her lips and they kissed deeply.

Bridget realised she was lost not much later. Just as lost as she'd been the night they'd first made love—only this time she was standing beside a paddock fence, with a couple of horses as spectators. But she didn't protest when he released her, only to take her hand and lead her back to the house.

Nor did she protest when she found herself in a round bedroom that might have been modelled on a traditional rondavel but was a symphony of sheer luxury. Beneath the soaring thatch roof, on the rich timber of a polished floor, stood a wooden four-poster bed with sheer white drapes. The coverlet was cream and the pillows lime-green. There were two beautiful sofas also in cream, with lime cushions, and wrought-iron candle sconces on the walls. The lamps were also fashioned of wrought-iron. The room felt exotic and slightly foreign, but it was breathtaking.

Even more breathtaking was the current that seemed to be flowing between her and Adam. She'd wondered at the back of her mind if the change of venue would stifle her urgent need of him—she was amazed at how urgent it had grown, when not that long ago she'd felt nothing but a sense of a partnership in the name of her baby.

Now, though, as he closed the door and took her in his arms again, the longing and thirst for him she'd escaped for a time in that strange little cocoon she'd inhabited became alive and vital. She breathed in the essence of him with a burgeoning feeling of joy.

She came alive beneath his wandering hands, and as he undressed her she returned the compliment. She undid his shirt buttons and slipped her arms around his waist.

'Mmm...' It was a sound of pure appreciation she made as she revelled in the long, lean, strong lines of him, and the feel of his shoulder beneath her cheek. But it wasn't only appreciation of the finer physical points of Adam Beaumont that prompted her appreciation. It wasn't only her growing desire and the waves of pleasure he was arousing in her.

It was that warm, safe feeling he'd given her once before, coming back...

'Not a scratch or a bruise,' he said as he ran his fingers down between her breasts. They were lying on the bed, their clothes were lying on the floor, and he'd drawn the bed's curtains, so they were isolated from the rest of the room—the rest of the world almost, she felt.

'No, all healed,' she agreed with an effort as his fingers returned to her nipples. 'That's too nice.'

He grinned—a sudden, wicked little grin. Then he sobered and lifted his head to rest it on his arm so he could look down at her. 'Too soon?' he asked, although his wandering hand drifted lower.

'Oh, no,' Bridget gasped, and clung to him suddenly. 'I might die if you don't...don't...'

'So might I, Mrs Smith. Shall we do it together?' He rolled onto her, and the lovely rhythm of two bodies as one commenced and grew to fever-pitch, which he sustained for longer than she would ever have believed possible. Then the slow drift back to reality came, but the closeness remained.

'That was—so—so…' She tried to talk when she was able to speak again, but she couldn't put it into words.

He pulled the linen sheet up over them and took her back in his arms. 'It was.' He paused, then said with suspicious gravity, 'I can't think of the right word either.'

She laughed softly and ran her hand over his shoulder then through his tousled hair, and finally laid it on his cheek. 'One of my fears—one of my *many* fears,' she said, and looked askance, 'has been laid to rest.'

'Only one?' he queried.

'Well, probably a lot of them,' she amended. 'But this was a really awkward one. I don't know if that's the right word—but I'll tell you all the same.'

His lips twisted. 'Go ahead.'

'Why are you laughing at me?' She took her hand away and looked hurt.

'If I am,' he replied, 'it's because it seems that, far from striking you speechless, I've had the opposite effect on you.'

'Oh.' Bridget digested this. 'Is it not the right etiquette to be talkative after sex—glorious sex?' She lowered her lashes so that he wouldn't see the glint of humour in her eyes.

'Now, that puts it in a nutshell—why didn't I think of putting it like that?' he asked wryly. 'Anyway, you may talk to your heart's content. I'm listening.'

Bridget suddenly grew quite serious, 'I was afraid that I'd only be able to do it if I'd thought I was going to die—like before. I know it sounds ridiculous, but there you go.'

'You did happen to mention something about dying,' he reminded her.

She looked rueful. 'Not that kind of dying—that's a different kind of death. You know what I mean.'

He studied the serious green depths of her eyes, and the perfect skin of her neck and shoulders, then stirred. 'Precisely, as it happens since I was in the same boat. But I think you're right. Can we lay the other fears to rest now?'

Bridget opened her mouth and closed it.

'What?' He kissed her forehead. 'You might as well tell me all of them.'

She grimaced. 'I thought…' she began, and hesitated, then plunged on, 'I thought that you would insist on all kinds of tests before you accepted this baby—if you accepted it, if you even wanted it.'

He shrugged. 'You can go through life being cynical and skeptical, but there comes a day when...I don't know...to have faith seems more rewarding.' He looked at her penetratingly.

'You can trust me on this one,' she said steadily.

He kissed her and ran his fingers through her hair, then walked them down her arm to her waist.

Bridget took a breath, but he grinned and kissed her again. 'Unfortunately we need to go. Do you mind? Otherwise we'll be flying in the dark.'

'Is it that late? No, of course not.'

But he took his time to kiss her and hug her thoroughly, before he threw back the sheet and they got up to have a shower.

As he was driving her back to her flat, he said, 'Will you come and have dinner with my uncle Julius tomorrow night?'

Bridget, who'd been in her own private little world, and still spiritually seemed to be at Mount Grace, came back to the present with an effort. 'Yes. If you like. Will you tell him?'

'That we're getting married? Yes. About the baby? That's up to you.'

'I think,' she said slowly, 'I'd like to keep that private for a while. It's still very early.'

'Fair enough. Look—' he brought his BMW to a halt '—I'd love to spend the evening with you, but I'm going to be playing catch up this evening and tomorrow as it is. Will you be OK?'

'I'll be fine,' she assured him. 'It has—it did turn out to be a lovely day,' she added quietly.

'It did.' He closed his fingers around hers. 'I'll pick you up tomorrow, around six-thirty.'

Bridget spent that night feeling a bit like Alice in Wonderland.

One thing had caused her to sigh with relief: there was a message on her answering machine from her mother. She'd be incommunicado for a few days, as they were going up country for a break.

But it did cause Bridget to wonder whether, even in a few days, she'd be able to explain things coherently to her mother.

It had all—finally—made sense to her at

the time, and in Adam's presence, but her mother could be a different matter.

She broke off her thoughts to bite her lip, and felt a little hot at the memory of being in Adam's presence. Then she realised that being alone in her apartment was another matter.

Alone in her apartment she was able to examine the events of the previous day in detail. Such as how she'd gone from anger, disbelief and hurt—from the conviction that she'd be far better off having her baby on her own—to allowing him to make love to her and loving every minute of it.

Would the Adam she remembered from the shed always have the power to seduce her?

And always be able to make her feel lonely and as if something precious was missing from her life when he wasn't there?

The other thing that perturbed her was the fact that she'd been able to take an impartial view of a woman Adam's brother had stolen from him—even offer advice on the subject— but now she could only think of her with a little bubble of dread.

She was ready when Adam pressed her doorbell.

She'd been to the hairdresser and had her

hair styled. She'd chosen a cropped jacket in a fine wool plaid, black on blue-green, over a short fitted black dress. With it she wore sheer black stockings and black suede shoes.

When she stared at herself in the mirror and thought she didn't look right—smart, yes, but too formal—she sternly took herself to task and refused, simply refused, to indulge in an orgy of redressing. Which was just as well, because Adam arrived early, bearing a bottle of French champagne.

His reaction was satisfying and vindicated that decision.

'How utterly elegant, Mrs Smith,' he murmured in the moments before he kissed her. 'And how wise to have waited to apply your lipstick,' he added, as he lifted his head with points of laugher dancing in his eyes.

'It's not that I waited. I just hadn't got around to it,' she denied. 'Truly! You're early.'

'I know,' he murmured, and pulled a long, slim box from the pocket of his beautiful grey suit, worn with a navy shirt. 'But I thought we might need a few minutes to sort this out.' He put the box and the bottle on the dining room table. 'Glasses?'

'Oh. I'll get them—but I shouldn't drink.'

He raised an eyebrow. 'Not even half a glass?'

Bridget moved into the kitchen and took two glasses out of a cupboard. She brought them back to the table as he expertly removed the foil and popped the cork. 'As a toast to us?' he added.

'Half a glass, then. Thank you.'

She accepted the champagne from him and they solemnly raised their glasses.

'To us,' he said.

'To us,' Bridget agreed, and took a sip.

'Open the box.'

Bridget hesitated. It couldn't be a ring box, it was too long, but it *was* obviously a jewellery box. Did she want jewellery from him? she found herself wondering.

She put her glass down and picked up the box. And she caught her breath as she flicked the catch. It wasn't a single ring box. There were four rings in it, all emeralds in different settings.

'I thought you might like to choose,' he said as she raised her stunned eyes to his. 'With those eyes I couldn't go past emeralds,' he murmured. 'But for the rest of it, it's up to you.'

Bridget dropped her gaze to the rings and licked her lips. 'They—they're all beautiful,' she said huskily. 'But I'm not sure I deserve an engagement ring like this—like these.'

'Why ever not?' he countered with a faint frown.

'I don't know,' she was forced to concede. 'I guess—perhaps I just wasn't expecting it.'

'Bridget.' He put his glass down on the table. 'We have an agreement. We have more than an agreement, don't we?'

She looked up at him to find him studying her intently. 'What do you mean?'

'We not only went through all the pros and cons yesterday, we also sealed it, I would have thought, in a way that was essentially romantic.'

'Well, yes, it was…' She trailed off and blushed as his blue gaze seemed to strip away her smart outfit and expose the slender curves of her body.

'So what's wrong with the next step being an engagement ring, and shortly a wedding ring?' he asked quietly, but with a glint of sheer—sheer what? she wondered. Sheer determination?

Her shoulders sagged suddenly, because it felt as if she'd walked into a battering ram and didn't know how to deal with it at all. Why should she feel there was anything to deal with over this issue? It was only an engagement ring. The much more telling circumstance was going to be whether she allowed him to put a wedding ring on her finger. But hadn't she banished that dilemma yesterday?

'More fears, Bridget?' he said.

'No. No. Uh…' she scanned the rings, and her fingers hovered over them. For some reason—because it might have been the least expensive?—it was the smallest she was drawn to: a baguette-cut central emerald flanked by two smaller round diamonds on a gold band. She took it out and slipped it onto her ring finger. It fitted perfectly, and seemed to be just right for the size and shape of her hand.

She studied it, holding it up to the light, admiring the green depths of the central stone and the fire of the two diamonds. 'This one,' she said.

'Don't you want to try the others?'

'No, thank you. This is—very lovely.'

'And very discerning of you, Mrs Smith,' he murmured as he closed the box on the other rings. 'It's the best emerald, and the diamonds are flawless.'

Bridget took a frustrated breath. 'Well, maybe I will try the others.'

'Why?'

'They may not be as expensive.'

He looked at her wryly. 'Too late—but take the ring off for a moment.'

Bridget did so, and handed it to him.

He picked up her hand. 'Bridget Tully-Smith, will you marry me?' He held the ring, poised to slip it back on her finger. 'I know I haven't exorcised all your fears,' he added. 'But I do believe it's what we should do, and I have your welfare very much at heart.'

It was the last thing Bridget had expected to burst into her mind at this point, but it did, and it articulated her deepest fear: she didn't want to be married for her welfare, she wanted to be married because he was deeply, hopelessly in love with her—*as she was with him.*

Her lips parted and her eyes darkened as the knowledge slammed into her heart, almost taking her breath away. How had this happened to her? she wondered a little desperately. In such a short time? Was it the wonderful sex? The fact that he'd saved her life a couple of times? No, not only that, she acknowledged. Love was the simple factor that explained why she wanted to be with him, why she felt lonely without him even when she felt like fighting him—or throwing grapes around because he frustrated her at times—it made no difference.

It was why she'd been restless and edgy all day, why she'd missed Adam Beaumont as she would always miss him when he was gone from her—and why it might be more than she could bear if she ever lost him… She loved him with all her heart.

'Bridget?'

He was frowning down at her, and she was forced to hide her inner amazement at what had happened to her, the storm of incredible self-knowledge that was so much more powerful than anything she'd ever experienced.

'Yes…' she said. What else could she say? 'I mean—*yes*.'

He slid the ring onto her finger and kissed

her lightly on the lips. 'Then why don't you put your lipstick on and we'll go and see my uncle Julius?'

She was quiet in the car, but he didn't seem to notice.

He did say, as he parked the car, 'Don't take any nonsense from my uncle.'

She looked at him, wide-eyed. 'What kind of nonsense?'

'He can be a pretty straight shooter. And this—' he switched off the engine and reached for her left hand to toy with the ring '—has come as a bit of a surprise to him.'

'Not only to him,' Bridget murmured.

'You mean your mother? Have you told her?'

'No.' Bridget explained about the message she'd received. 'But I was actually thinking of me. I feel a little shell-shocked. And I'm not sure if I feel like facing—anyone.'

'He's not well, Bridget. His doctors reckon he's living on borrowed time. But he's important to me, and I know this will mean a lot to him—the thought of me being settled.' He grimaced and released her hand, but took her chin in his fingers so he could look into her eyes.

'What if he doesn't like me?'

'What's not to like?' he queried, his lips twisting. 'Trust me, he'll like you. Just be yourself.'

Julius Beaumont stared at Bridget, then at Adam in turn, his bushy white eyebrows almost up to his hairline. 'Well, well, well,' he said. 'This is an unexpected pleasure, young lady. Sit down and tell me about yourself. All I got from Adam were the bare facts.'

Bridget relaxed a little, and she exchanged a little glance with Adam that Julius correctly interpreted as containing relief on her part and encouragement on his.

So, Julius found himself thinking, there *is* a bond of some kind between them. Not that I really believed he went out and chose the first girl he could find—or did I? Adam was a mixture of inspired long-term insight and the odd completely off-the-cuff, out-of-the-blue action…

'Thank you,' Bridget said, mercifully unaware of these thoughts, but warming to the old man. She sank onto a settee next to the

wheelchair and accepted a glass of juice from
Adam, who handed his great-uncle the one
Scotch he was allowed.

'Tell me how you met?' Julius continued.

Bridget did so, leaving out the finer points.
'He saved my life—not once but twice,' she
finished simply.

Julius Beaumont sipped his Scotch as his
internal musing ran on... Not a bad begin-
ning. In fact a whole lot better than he'd hoped
for! 'Go on,' he encouraged. 'Tell me about
yourself,' he repeated.

And then Bridget surprised him even further—but she also surprised herself, as his
horse paintings caught her eye and dredged
something up from the back of her mind,
something she could share with this old
man.

She said whimsically, 'I haven't done a
whole lot with my life yet, although that could
be about to change, but I believe we might
have something in common. I can tell you
the last twenty Melbourne Cup winners in
chronological order.'

Not only Julius but Adam Beaumont stared
at her in surprise.

'My father was fanatical about thoroughbreds,' Bridget went on. 'It was his hobby. Not that he was much of a gambler. Ten dollars each way was his maximum bet, but it was impossible to live in the same house with him and not imbibe some of that fanaticism.' She paused and her lips curved into a smile. 'And because my birthday is in the first week of November—Cup time—we used to study the Cup form together and he'd put an extra ten dollars on our choice for me, for my birthday present.'

'How often did you win?' Adam asked with a chuckle.

'Not always, of course, but over the years I totalled quite a nice, tidy sum.'

'Then you'd better come and study the form with me!' Julius remarked enthusiastically. 'My record has been abysmal lately.' He turned to Adam. 'Did you know this about this girl?' he barked.

'No,' Adam confessed. 'She keeps surprising me.'

Better and better! Julius thought, as Mervyn came to call them to dinner.

Before they sat down to eat, there was a surprise waiting for Bridget in the dining room. A wall of pictures that might have been gold-framed and artistically placed but weren't actually paintings. They were photos of Melbourne Cup winners.

And Julius Beaumont wasn't content to start his meal until she'd pinpointed all the ones she'd won on!

The meal flowed smoothly, and the conversation didn't flag.

But Bridget did look a little tired at the end of it, and Adam asked her in a quiet aside if she was all right.

She nodded, but he slipped her hand into his as they stood to say their farewells, and promised to come back soon.

Julius saw that little gesture, and it was on his mind after they'd left. Although there had been no other lover-like gestures, Adam did care about her welfare, he thought. And the absence of anything else lover-like might just have been a matter of good taste, he mused. In fact there had been a lot of good taste about Bridget Tully-Smith, he reflected. No pretensions, no bravado, her own nails, no excessive make-up. In all probability a thoroughly nice girl.

So what could go wrong?

A face swam into his mind's eye: Marie-Claire Beaumont's. A flawlessly beautiful face, he had to admit, even although he didn't like the girl.

And it frustrated him unbearably for a moment to think that there was no way he could keep Adam and Marie-Claire apart if they chose otherwise.

But there is something I can do, he said to himself. If you think I'm going to tamely accept *all* your dictates, Adam Beaumont, think again. He rang the bell for Mervyn.

'You called?' Mervyn stuck his head around the lounge door. 'Ready for bed?'

'No, I am not, Merv.' Julius was the only one who had the temerity to shorten Mervyn's name. 'Get me my solicitor.'

Mervyn came fully into the room. 'You want to speak to him?'

'No, I want to dance the Irish Jig with him—of course I want to speak to him,' Julius said testily. 'Here. In person.'

Mervyn consulted the grandfather clock. 'It's ten o'clock. He may be in bed.'

'Then get him out of bed! And don't you go anywhere. I may need you.'

'I do live here,' Mervyn pointed out. 'And

I don't think it's a good idea to get worked up over anything. We could regret it, you know.'

'Just do as you're told, Merv!' Julius ordered. 'And stop calling me *we*. It drives me insane. Pour me a Scotch while you're about it.'

'No,' Mervyn said. 'That I do refuse to do.'

CHAPTER SEVEN

BRIDGET stirred the next morning and discovered herself to be loosely wrapped in Adam's arms in her own bed.

'That's brilliant,' she murmured as she revelled in it.

He opened one eye. 'I haven't done anything.'

'You don't have to. You did enough last night. I'm enjoying things just as they are.'

He touched his forefinger to her mouth. 'You're easy to please.' He hugged her, then hitched the pillows up and sat back against them. They were both naked beneath the sheet and coverlet. She snuggled up against him and rested her cheek on his chest.

He stroked her hair. 'You were inspired last night with my uncle.'

'That was pure fluke. Seeing his horse

paintings reminded me of what you'd told me about his passion for the Melbourne Cup.' She paused. 'I liked him.'

'He liked you.'

'You could tell?' she queried.

'Yes. What do you want to do today?'

Bridget sat up. 'You have a day off?' she asked, on a note of excitement.

He fluffed her fringe up with his fingers. 'Yes. Well, I'm taking one anyway. I thought we could—'

'Why did you ask me what I wanted to do if you've already got something in mind?' she broke in, and eyed him sternly.

'I…' He paused and rubbed the blue shadows on his jaw, then shrugged. 'You go ahead. I must tell you that you look like a disapproving governess, though.' His lips quirked.

'And I'll tell you about my parents. My father used to drive my mother mad doing something very similar.'

'He did?'

She nodded solemnly.

'What?' he asked, with an expression of mock fear.

'He used to say to her "We can do A or

B. It's up to you." Then, when she chose B, say, he would agree, but add the rider that on the other hand A would be the more sensible choice, leaving her in no doubt that A was what he'd always wanted to do. "Why didn't you just come out and say so?" she would cry in frustration.'

'Ah. All right. What would *you* like to do today, Bridget?' he asked with elaborate courtesy.

Bridget pretended to mull over the possibilities. 'There is one thing,' she said at last. 'I'd just like to spend the day with you. That's all.'

'You're a tease, Mrs Smith,' he said ruefully. 'Well, I had this thought. Since I spend all my spare time up at Mount Grace, I don't actually have a house on the Coast. I stay in hotels. So I thought we might look around for one—a house, not a hotel. Somewhere you'd be happy to call home while we're not up there. The question is, though, would you like a house or an apartment?'

'If by an apartment you mean a penthouse in the sky,' Bridget said thoughtfully, 'I think I'd rather have a house. Seems more appropriate for a child, and I'm not a fan of having to get into a lift every time you want to go out. It's also nice to have grass beneath your feet— I can't believe I'm saying this.' She looked conscience-struck.

'Why not? It makes sense.'

'Yes, but it's—well, I'm sure there's going to be an awful lot of money involved—your money—and it's going to be such a change of lifestyle for me.' Her eyes widened at the thought.

'Talking about a change of lifestyle...' He put his hand gently on her tummy beneath the sheet. 'When is this baby due?'

She told him a date in December. 'But that's by my reckoning. I haven't seen a doctor yet.'

'OK. That's something else we can do today.'

'Oh, but we might not get an appointment!'

'With my doctor, we will,' he said with a lurking grin.

'Life is so much simpler when you're a millionaire,' she responded with a faint frown. 'Nothing ever seems to stand in your way.'

'Things do, believe me.'

'Large things, maybe, but not small things?' she suggested.

He shrugged, but didn't comment on that. He said instead, 'We also have to set a wedding date.'

'Not today, we don't,' Bridget heard herself say. 'We have plenty of time for that.'

'But since we *are* getting married we may as well—in the next few days at least,' he replied.

She was silent as she grappled with a feeling she'd experienced before in relation to Adam Beaumont—the feeling that she was up against a battering ram. Yet since she *had* agreed to marry him, and since she *was* pregnant, what was the point in delaying it?

But it was a lot more than that, wasn't it? Last night she'd been struck by the knowledge that she'd fallen deeply in love with him. Last night she'd gone to bed with him willingly and loved every minute of it. Especially since she had been tired and a bit strung-up, so had really appreciated the gently warm experience he'd made it rather than the fireworks of the last time they'd slept together.

She articulated the thought that had been

at the back of her mind ever since all this had come up. 'Let me tell my mother first.'

'Is she liable to change your mind?'

Bridget hesitated. 'She's liable to preach caution.'

He sat up abruptly and eased her up beside him. 'It's too late for that, Bridget.'

She said nothing, but pleated the sheet between her fingers.

'I know it's all a huge change for you...' He paused and studied the top of her head. 'But the sooner we get it under way, the sooner you'll get used to it and the easier it's going to be for you.'

She looked up at last, but he couldn't read her eyes.

'You don't rewrite your life without some upheavals,' he said quietly.

'I suppose not.' But she didn't sound entirely convinced. 'Is it not going to be a rather huge upheaval for you too?'

'Of course. But I'm looking forward to it more and more. And our own place—our very own, one you can fit out to your heart's content—will help.'

She looked around and thought of Mount Grace. She had to agree. Her mother's shadow seemed to hover over her in *this* flat; his mother's ghost—much as she'd fallen in love with Mount Grace—had to linger there.

She came to a sudden decision. 'All right. I'll look at houses with you, and I'll see your doctor today. But I'd still like to speak to my mother—no,' she said as he moved restlessly. 'I'm not going to let her change my mind, but I would like her to be here for the wedding, so any date needs to be one she can fit in with.'

'So long as it's not too far away.'

Bridget temporized, but he took her in his arms and lay back with her, fitting the curves of her body into the lean planes and angles of his. 'How right does that feel?' he queried, with a wicked little glint in his eyes as he cupped her breast.

'That feels like pure blackmail,' she replied, but a little breathlessly.

'It is,' he agreed. 'You seem to have brought out a pirate-like streak in me, Mrs Smith. Is that the right word?' he mused.

'Pirate-like? Well, devious also springs to mind.'

He kissed the tip of her nose.

'I give up,' she said on a gurgle of laughter. 'You're a hard man to say no to, Mr Beaumont.'

* * *

A little later, far from feeling drowsy, Adam got energetically out of bed and announced that he was starving.

'Ah,' she said, curling up in his space. 'Yesterday I experimented with black tea and dry toast, and I didn't have any morning sickness, so I think I may stick to that. I don't think I should even *think* about cooking breakfast.'

'Don't worry, I'll take care of it all—including the black tea.' He headed for the shower.

'You cook?' Bridget asked with a tinge of surprise.

He turned back to her. 'In a limited sort of way. I spent a year after school jackerooing on a cattle station in the Northern Territory. Bacon and eggs is one of my strengths. Damper is another, but I'll make do with bread this morning. Do you have any plum jam?'

'Er—no. Do you like it?'

'I became addicted to it on damper. We used to get it in big tins and, apart from sugar, it was just about the only sweet thing we got.'

'How about strawberry jam?' she asked gravely.

He grinned. 'That'll do.'

'So that's where you got your expertise with ropes and axes and so on? Jackerooing?' she hazarded.

'Yes.' He grimaced. 'Such as it is.'

On his way to the shower he stopped and studied a painting on the wall—one of hers. A delicate study of some coral-pink ixora blooms on a velvety midnight background.

He turned back to her. 'I thought you said you weren't any good?'

'I'm average,' she answered.

'I disagree. In fact, I would be surprised if your new career *isn't* based on art. Have you started painting yet?'

She shook her head. 'I haven't had time.'

He squinted at the tiny initials in the corner—B T-S—then went to take his shower.

Bridget stayed cuddled up in bed and listened to him singing snatches of a sea shanty in a pleasant, husky voice.

It brought her a feeling of real contentment, although she smiled to herself to think of him as a closet shower singer. But *he* must be feeling contented, at least, she reasoned, even if she wasn't the love of his life…

She saw his doctor later in the day, and had her pregnancy officially confirmed. She also saw a number of houses, and fell in love with one of them.

It was on the Nerang River, behind Surfers Paradise, so it was peaceful but central. It had a lovely garden and a jetty, but it needed some TLC—mostly only cosmetic, so it wouldn't be a time-consuming exercise. She specifically asked not to be told how much it cost, although she knew that its position alone would guarantee a hefty price tag.

Inwardly, she discerned that she was a little uneasy about this house—to the extent that she did say to Adam that they had months up their sleeve and didn't need to rush into anything.

He simply shrugged—and told her the next day that it was signed and sealed.

The next evidence she got of his determination to get his own way was over her job. She still had nearly two weeks' leave in front of her, but happened casually to mention when she'd be going back to work.

Why not quit now and get it over with? had been his response. Why not start painting now?

She'd hesitated, and he'd reminded her that she'd been having second thoughts about it anyway. He'd also let drop that Julia had moved overseas.

'Did you have anything to do with that?'

They were dining out at a chic Italian café. The tablecloths were red, with green over-cloths, the glassware sparkled, the air was redolent with tantalising aromas, and the menu offered a delicious variety of pasta. It all faded into the background, though, as Bridget was unable to mask her surprise at this news.

He toyed with his wine glass. 'Yes.'

'How so?'

'I managed to get her a job in Singapore.'

'Why didn't you tell me? Did you coerce her?'

He rubbed his jaw. 'To a certain extent. I pointed out to her that spreading unsub-stantiated rumours was not something to be viewed lightly.'

'They were true,' Bridget said.

'Not at the time, they weren't,' he said flatly.

'Your brother—' Bridget began, but he broke in.

'Look, Bridget, Henry is a married man with two children.' He gestured. 'I'm not making excuses for him, but Julia was always on shaky ground there. Don't you agree?' And he raised an eyebrow at her.

'I suppose so,' she said slowly. 'Is she all right? You must have threatened her with—something.'

'We did a deal. Materially, she drove a fairly hard bargain. But it's actually a much more challenging job there than doing the social rounds here.'

Bridget digested this for a long moment. They were both casually dressed, she in jeans and a blouse that matched her eyes, he in jeans and a sports jacket over a round-necked T-shirt. But it crossed her mind to think that whatever he wore these days, and even if his hair *was* wind-ruffled from their earlier stroll on the beach, there was no disguising that he was a powerful man. Capable of a lot more than railroading Julia Nixon out of town— and he had railroaded her, even if he had got her a better job.

And not only powerful, she thought, as something Julia had once said about him popped into her mind—he was as sexy as hell. She'd been so right. Apart from her own intimate knowledge of him, Bridget couldn't fail to by struck by the reaction of women who came in contact with him—or were simply sitting a few tables away from him, as one was now. She couldn't keep her eyes off him...

And it all caused her unease to surface again. What chance did she have of fighting him if he ever became minded to use his power against her?

'Did she mention me?'

'Yes.' He paused, looking completely unamused. 'She told me to get out of your life. It was advice I declined.'

'Do you still want to gain control of Beaumonts?' Bridget said slowly.

'Oh, yes.' He twirled some pasta round his fork. 'But not thanks to Julia Nixon.'

'So—so you've done nothing to take advantage of these rumours she spread?'

He smiled lethally. 'I've been sitting on my hands, you could say, other than persuading her to leave town. But the right moment will come.'

Bridget said no more on the subject, but it occurred to her that Beaumont Minerals was a factor she shouldn't discount in her relationship with Adam Beaumont, for the simple reason that it might mean more to him than anything.

The next day she sat down and wrote a long e-mail to her mother, who still had not returned from her 'few days' little break. She didn't send it, though.

She was aware that her mother had a rather vague concept of time. She remembered that both her mother and her new husband were keen amateur archaeologists, and she could imagine them on some dig, miles from anywhere, quite oblivious of the passage of time.

But, although she wanted particularly to speak to her mother, in some ways it was easier to lay the facts out in an e-mail, and she filed it in her 'drafts' folder, so as to have it on hand when she did speak to her. At the same time, seeing those facts laid out did make her stop and ponder her new life. And ponder, specifically, the speed with which it was all happening to her. Not only that, she was still unsure what to do about her job.

From a couple of remarks he'd let fall she knew Adam was getting more and more impatient about setting a wedding date. In fact, indirectly, they would have their first serious falling-out over it…

He rang her one morning and invited her to a dinner that night…

'What kind of dinner?'

'Formal, black tie,' he said down the line, and named a five-star restaurant she'd heard of but never been to, which happened to be in the hotel where he was staying. 'It's a business dinner, and most of the other guests will be Korean. I'm working with a Korean consortium at the moment on a construction project.'

'That doesn't give me a lot of time,' she said slowly.

'Doing anything else today?'

She bit her lip. 'No. When you say formal, do you mean long dress?'

'Yes. Is that a problem?'

Bridget came to the decision that she wouldn't be bested by a wardrobe deficiency. 'Not at all.'

'That's my girl. Look, if I don't get there myself, Trent will pick you up at seven and deliver you to me. See you!' And he rang off.

So, she thought, that's how high-flying businessmen do things. I wonder who he would have taken if it wasn't me? I wonder if it's some kind of test to see how I stack up against his high-flying business associates?

She stopped as this thought crossed her mind, and shortly took herself shopping.

It was Trent who was standing outside her door when the bell rang at seven, and he did the most gratifying double-take.

'Oh, do forgive me, Miss Tully-Smith,' he said ruefully, 'but you look absolutely stunning!'

Bridget looked down at herself. Rather than an evening dress, she wore fitted slim-line ivory taffeta pants, very high latest-fashion silver shoes and a silver spangled loose top over an ivory camisole. Her coppery hair was styled and bouffant, her nails were painted to match her glossy lips—she'd toyed with the idea of black nail varnish but decided against it—and the only jewellery she wore was her engagement ring. Her eyes were a clear, sparkling green.

'Thank you, Trent,' she said. 'But will it

be appropriate, do you think? I wasn't quite sure.'

'Ma'am, you'll blow them away,' Trent assured her.

It was a view Adam seemed to share when she arrived at his suite. He was wearing black trousers, a white dress shirt and an undone black bow tie, and his dinner jacket was hanging over the back of a chair. His dark hair was tamed and tidy.

He put the phone down as she came in, and whistled softly.

'Oh, thank you!' She beamed at him. 'Every dress I tried on seemed to make me look—portly.'

His eyebrows shot up. 'Portly?'

She nodded gravely. 'I can't see any difference in my figure, but there must be some because that's how they made me feel.'

'I could give you my considered opinion,' he offered, 'but that would involve a minute inspection—and, of course, undressing you.'

A tide of pink rose into Bridget's cheeks as his blue gaze wandered up and down her. 'Er—thank you, but I don't think I'll...need that.'

He glanced at his watch. 'We have half an hour.'

Her colour deepened. 'You're not serious?'

'I couldn't think of anything I'd rather do at this moment in time.'

Their gazes clashed, and Bridget was assailed by a vivid image of his hands on her body as he undressed her item by item; by a breathtaking image of the tall, lean length of him also unclothed and intent on reducing her to a quivering state of desire. Not playfully, as he sometimes did it, but silently, and with all the erotic force he could bring to it.

'Adam...' She took a shaky little breath. 'If you mean what I think you mean, that—that—' she looked down at herself and gestured eloquently with both hands '—that would *wreck* me!'

There was a suspended moment when she felt she might almost cut the tide of suspense laced with longing that flowed between.

Then he grinned wickedly and held out his hand. 'Come here.'

She went reluctantly, unsure of what to expect.

'May I make a date to...if not wreck you,

definitely undress you and make love to you after this dinner, Mrs Smith?'

She laughed in relief and leant against him. 'You may, Mr Beaumont.'

The dinner was a success.

Bridget held her own amongst the fifty or so guests, and was much complimented on her appearance—often in broken English, but the sentiments were obviously genuine. Any surprise that Adam Beaumont had acquired a fiancée was well hidden, but many of the guests were only business acquaintances and came from the other side of the world anyway. They might not even have understood the situation.

When they returned to his suite she was happy with the way things had gone, and a little surprised to realise how nervous she'd been about this event.

He poured himself a nightcap, and she had a cup of black tea and then yawned prodigiously. 'I should think about going home.'

He looked at her askance. 'What's wrong with staying here?'

She hesitated. 'I don't think I'd feel right about that.'

'Bridget.' He put his glass down and pulled off his bow tie. 'We are engaged.'

'I know, but—well, I didn't bring anything with me.'

'What does that matter? There are enough toiletries, shampoos, robes, and heaven knows what here for six people, let alone two.'

Bridget mulled over this. 'But you see,' she said at last, 'I would have to go home tomorrow wearing this.' She looked down at herself, at her spangled evening top, taffeta pants and high-heeled shoes. 'That would look—funny.'

'Nonsense. No one would give two hoots.'

She tilted her chin at him. 'I would.'

His lips twitched, then a tinge of impatience came to his eyes. 'You could get into the lift and go straight down to the car park.'

'Who knows who else could get into the lift?'

His nostrils flared as he took an irritated breath.

'Then I could send out for some clothes for you tomorrow morning.'

'Send who? Trent? No, thank you.'

He made a gruff little sound in his throat. 'Bridget, if you'd agree to move in with me—come to that, if you'd stop fluffing around and marry me—none of this would happen. Besides which, you promised.' He looked her up and down significantly.

She turned pink. 'You could come home with me,' she suggested.

'It is one o'clock in the morning. We're halfway across town.' He looked at her derisively.

Bridget rose and picked up her silver-beaded purse. 'Then I'll go alone. Incidentally, I'm not *fluffing* around, and I'm not even that sure that I *will* marry you, Adam!'

And she marched towards the door.

He caught her before she reached it, and detained her with his hands around her waist. 'I had no idea you were such a puritan,' he murmured. 'Although I should have known you had a temper.'

'Not only that,' she responded, her eyes flashing, 'but I've lost the mood—so please let me go.'

'I haven't. Lost the mood,' he elucidated. 'But here's a suggestion. What say that tomorrow morning I call down to the boutique in the foyer and get them to send up a selection of clothes for you? They don't even need to see you—you can leave here dressed as you see fit. I really don't understand what difference it makes, leaving in daytime clothes, but since it's so dear to your heart—'

He stopped and caught her wrist as she went to slap his face.

'Don't, Bridget,' he warned, on a cool, dangerous note.

'I'll tell you what difference it makes,' she said through her teeth. 'I wouldn't look so highly conspicuous. I wouldn't look like some good-time girl after a one-night stand. I'd look ordinary and un-noteworthy.'

He shrugged. 'Then we're agreed on this course of action?'

'Yes. No! I *really* don't like you for not understanding, and—'

But he pulled her into his arms and started to kiss her. She fought him briefly but it was a losing battle, especially when he lifted his head briefly to say, 'I'm sorry. I should have understood. I will try to be more understanding in the future.'

Despite the little glint of sheer devilry in his eyes, she felt herself melting...

'Was I silly?'

Bridget asked the question about an hour

later, when she was lying beside him on the bed in a pool of golden lamplight, having been exquisitely made love to.

'Don't answer,' she went on, and smoothed her fingers through his hair. 'I'm talking to myself. I'm just trying to judge how legitimate my reaction was. In light of the fact that I will *still* be leaving here tomorrow morning—this morning—having spent the night with you.'

He kissed the bare curve of her shoulder. 'I wouldn't worry about it.'

'But I do. I mean, I like to have things clear in my own mind. It just…' She paused and thought for a moment. 'It just occurred to me that it could be really embarrassing—especially if I met anyone I know.'

'I can see that. Now,' he said gravely.

'Is it going to be any less embarrassing wearing jeans and a jumper, though?' she mused.

'Bridget.' He sat up, and couldn't go on for a moment because he was laughing. Then, 'If we make it a respectable time of the day, if you hold on to the thought that we *are* engaged, it should be a breeze. And I agree with you—you would have looked rather conspicuous in evening dress. Happy now?'

She snuggled up to him. 'Yes.'

'Now, I still have something to do—an inspection to make,' he reminded her. 'Although you don't feel at all portly to me.'

She bore his 'inspection' with equanimity at first. But when he announced that there was only one change he could see, and his fingers stilled on her nipples, she had to draw several breaths to maintain her composure.

'These are different,' he said, stroking and plucking. 'Darker. But it's a very fine difference.'

'It's a very short time. Out of nine months, I mean,' she said with an effort.

'Still, time marches on,' he murmured, and she held her breath this time, quite sure he was going to make some remark about them getting married.

He didn't. He drew her close to him and kissed the top of her head, and started to make love to her again. She responded to the warmth and security of his arms and his body, to the pleasure he brought her, with a warmth and a bestowing of pleasure of her own. And she wondered, at the same time, why she didn't just marry him as soon as he wanted?

It is the one thing I can hold out about, she answered herself. It is the one thing—even although I've agreed to it—I can choose to do when I feel ready. And I know I don't want to keel over like a pack of cards over everything.

The next few days seemed to fly by.

They ate out a lot—once even going up to Mount Tamborine for lunch, in a fabulous garden restaurant. He also took her, wearing a hard hat and a fluorescent green overshirt, up one of his buildings in progress, via the outside construction lift. She gasped at the view from the top, and stopped to think about how highly successful he was.

She hadn't reversed her decision to not move into his hotel—another small holding-out against Adam Beaumont—so he'd moved some of his clothes and gear to her flat, although he still occasionally spent the night at his hotel.

When he did stay with her she discovered that he never went to bed before midnight, yet was always up by six. And he always went for a body surf or, if there was no surf, swam or jogged. And if she thought he was beautiful dressed in a tailored suit, he was even more so when he came back from those early-morning excursions, with his hair all ruffled, his jaw blue with stubble and his body cold and fresh.

'That's my axeman,' she said to him one morning, when he sat down on the side of the bed and pulled her into his arms hungrily.

'That's my essential Mrs Smith,' he replied. 'Not soaked to the skin, but with no make up, et cetera, and quite *au naturel*.'

One morning he came home with a dog.

'What's this?' she enquired, as the woolly, curly, cream and quite large dog followed him into the flat and sat down composedly.

'This is Rupert, according to his collar, although there's no other information. I found him on the beach, alone and possibly lost. I have not been able to detach him from my side since then.'

'But—well—' Bridget started to laugh. 'What are you going to do with him?'

'I was hoping you would offer to ring up the RSPCA and ask them to come and

deal with him. He could be micro-chipped.
Unfortunately—' he consulted his watch
'—I'm running really late for a meeting
now, so I won't be able to be of much assis-
tance.'

Rupert had other ideas, however. He po-
sitioned himself outside the bathroom door
while Adam showered, and Bridget tried to
get hold of the RSPCA. But it was too early
for them except in cases of dire emergency,
as she told Adam.

He knotted his tie and scooped his keys into
his pocket. 'This could be an emergency,' he
said. 'Would you be a darling and look after
him until they can take over?'

Bridget eyed the dog, now sitting at Adam's
feet. 'Yes, if he agrees.'

'He's only a dog.'

'I know, but I just have a feeling he's attached himself to you.'

In the event, Rupert had. Because when
Adam left he sat beside the front door and
emitted ear-piercing yowls of complete dev-
astation.

Adam came back in.

'What are we going to do?' Bridget asked
helplessly. 'The neighbours... Anyway, I

don't think you're allowed to have dogs in this building.'

Adam shrugged. 'I'll take him with me. Trent can look after him and sort things out.'

They left together, Adam and the dog, and Bridget was struck by a fit of giggles as she watched from the window as Adam loaded the dog into the passenger seat of his shiny BMW. Rupert accepted his status as number one passenger with aplomb and sat upright, staring ahead.

She was subject to similar fits of laughter on and off for the rest of the day. And never more so than when they returned, together, at about five o'clock.

'What's this?' she asked, as another gust of laughter shook her.

Adam glanced at the dog. 'Well may you ask—and it's no laughing matter. He tried to bite Trent, and he refused to have anything to do with the RSPCA. I drew the line at a containment net and a tranquilising dart.'

'So?'

Adam threw his car keys onto the dining table and shrugged out of his jacket. 'So I took him to my meeting. I took him to three meetings. He was perfectly well-behaved so long as he could sit at my feet and get taken for a walk now and then—I need a drink.'

'I'm not surprised,' she managed to say, having extreme difficulty in keeping a straight face.

'I know you're still laughing,' he accused, 'but have you any idea how traumatised my whole office is? I had the girls crying because they didn't want to see him hurt. I thought Trent was going to give notice on the spot. And I now own gifts pressed on me by those same girls: a dog basket, a set of bowls, a *huge* bag of dog biscuits.'

Bridget handed him a Scotch. 'There, there,' she said soothingly, and the front doorbell rang.

It was an RSPCA officer, together with a couple and a boy of about ten.

Rupert barked joyously and jumped up to lick the boy's face. The boy buried his face in the curly cream fur.

'So that's all sorted,' the officer said. 'They don't know how he came to get lost, but they're new to the area so that probably explains it.'

Before he left, Rupert came back to Adam and sat down in front of him.

Adam scratched the fur beneath his chin. 'I have to say it hasn't all been a breeze, mate, but you're a very fine dog.'

And, almost as if he understood every word, Rupert licked his hand then bounded over to his young master's side.

Bridget closed the door on them all, and Adam, with a sigh, sank down onto her settee. 'I must be a laughing-stock,' he said ruefully.

Bridget sat down beside him and snuggled up to him. 'On the contrary. There's obviously something very, very loveable about you.'

He put his arm round her shoulders and glanced at her with a wicked little glint. 'So you've noticed?'

'In the face of such canine devotion I could hardly fail to.'

'When are you going to marry me, then?'

Bridget sobered. 'I still haven't heard from my mother.'

'If we were to set the date for a fortnight from today, surely she'd be able to make it?'

'I—I guess so.'

'Well, why don't you start thinking about dresses and honeymoons and the like?'

* * *

Was that when it all started to tumble down like the house of cards it really was? Bridget was to wonder later.

She'd agreed to the fortnight time limit, and she'd asked what kind of wedding it would be. He'd told her with a lurking grin that it was up to her, but how did quiet, simple and very private sound?

'There you go again,' she'd accused. 'Giving me no choices!' But she'd almost immediately confessed that quiet, simple and private sounded fine to her.

She had, she saw later, still been caught up in the warmth and amusement of that day. She'd been convinced she loved Adam Beaumont—especially the very human side of him she'd witnessed that day.

She'd smothered the deep-seated reservations she had about marrying him, about rushing into things—or being rushed into things as if she were on a runaway train. She'd buried the instinct that had told her to hold back. It wasn't something she fully understood, anyway.

But the very next day it had become clearer.

Marie-Claire Beaumont announced her

separation from her husband, Henry, citing irreconcilable differences. The couple's two children, four and two, had moved out of the family home with their mother, so it was reported in the paper.

It was noted in the same article that some Beaumont shareholders were calling for an immediate meeting of the company's troubled board. And, although no parallel was drawn to deserting a sinking ship, if you read between the lines you could make the inference that the timing of this separation might have wider implications than two people who'd fallen out of love.

Since Adam had gone to Adelaide on a business trip, Bridget was unable to judge what kind of turmoil this announcement might have brought him. But she was in no doubt about the kind of turmoil it brought to her.

That hidden, mysterious little instinct buried in her psyche stood up well and truly now to be counted. What did this woman really mean to Adam? You couldn't love a man and not wonder about it, she saw. She might have been able to mostly ignore the question while Marie-Claire was safely married to his brother—or so she'd thought—but if she divorced Henry and was free…?

Had this been on the cards anyway? *Did* they have irreconcilable differences, Henry and Marie-Claire? Or was she deserting a sinking ship? Had Julia contributed, with all her bitterness?

And when Adam did come home, two days later, it was impossible to gauge his real state of mind on the issue. She might not have been able to anyway, she acknowledged. She was quite sure he was a master at hiding his feelings.

But what brought him home was traumatic anyway: the death of his great-uncle Julius, who had passed away peacefully in his sleep.

'I'm so sorry,' Bridget said down the line to Adam when he rang her with the news. 'I'm *so* sorry. I know he meant a lot to you.'

'Thank you,' he replied briefly. 'The funeral is the day after tomorrow. Will you come?'

'Yes, of course. If you want me to.'

'Why wouldn't I?' he countered, rather harshly.

Bridget took a breath. 'I wasn't sure whether

anyone knew about us—apart from your uncle, of course. And some Korean business-men. And Trent.'

'My uncle was the only one of the rest who mattered, but it's time everyone knew,' he said. 'Bridget, I'll be back tomorrow morning.' His voice softened. 'Take care of yourself in the meantime.'

'I will,' she promised, but she was disturbed when she put down the phone.

Did she want to go on show to the whole world at such a sad event? Who would be there? Surely there would be no wedding preparations now? No wedding, come to that, so soon after his uncle's passing? Not that she had done anything yet…

Marie-Claire Beaumont was at the funeral, surprisingly at her husband's side, and she was impossible to ignore—she was that kind of woman.

She was tall, with long fair hair and exqui-site grey eyes. Black became her beautifully, and her designer suit with its short skirt set off her sleek figure and long legs.

No surprises there, Bridget thought. She'd already known this woman was something special, but had she anticipated that her looks, her elegance, her composure—not to mention, of course, her history—would force her gaze to return to her again and again?

When she realised this was happening, Bridget took herself to task and thought instead of Melbourne Cup winners. She herself had chosen to wear the same outfit she'd worn to dinner with Julius Beaumont, and that helped to bring back the only time she'd met the old man.

But she couldn't help also studying Henry Beaumont. Julia had been right. He was as tall and good-looking as Adam, but there was a difference. It took some time for Bridget to put her finger on it, and then it came to her that, while Adam Beaumont had an inner stillness that translated to a harnessed kind of power, Henry looked discontented. He had a curious unfulfilled quality about him, and he looked older than the four years older than Adam she knew him to be.

The wake was held in Julius's apartment, with Mervyn in command of a discreet army of caterers. Champagne flowed, and the red velvet curtains were swept aside on the stunning view of the ocean from Narrowneck at its best, calm and blue and stretching for ever.

The wake started out quietly, but soon the hubbub of conversation rose and the temperature grew too, as many, many people came to celebrate Julius's life now they'd mourned his death. And there were plenty of raised eyebrows as Adam introduced Bridget as his fiancée.

But perhaps the sheer press of people would shield her from too much attention—and anyway, there was Marie-Claire.

Had she always been such a scene-stealer? Bridget wondered. Or did it just come naturally? It might even be a form of bravado—it was to be noted that she and Henry were always on opposite sides of the room...

But when she was presented to Bridget there was more than bravado to Marie-Claire. She raised her eyebrows and smiled quite gently. Apart from a murmured 'How do you do?' she said nothing to Bridget at all, but the look she bestowed on Adam was a clear challenge, and what she said next was a clear invitation.

She said, in a fascinating, lilting voice, 'Despite today's solidarity for Julius's sake, you probably didn't think I'd do it, did you, Adam? But I have, darling—oh, I have—and now I'm on my own.'

And she moved away, but Bridget could literally feel the tension in the man standing at her side...

Those words might have meant anything, but to Bridget they contained a clear message. She must believe I don't know anything about her, she thought in a stunned kind of way as new arrivals presented themselves and she shook several hands and said she knew not what.

Not only that, her incredulous thoughts ran on, but she mustn't think I'm any threat, anything to take seriously, even although Adam and I are engaged...

Her thoughts ran along these lines for another twenty minutes or so, until she knew she couldn't go on any longer. She asked Adam if he'd mind if she went home.

He immediately looked concerned. 'What's wrong? Feeling sick?'

'No—not yet, anyway. But I'm *hot*, and I know—I know you can't leave, but I could get a taxi. Please?' she added.

He frowned. 'You could rest here in one

of the bedrooms. There's the will to be read after—'

'No,' Bridget broke in urgently. 'I really want to go home, so I can get changed and comfortable,' she insisted, and tried to smile. 'I'll be fine.'

She must have convinced him, but even so he came downstairs and put her into a taxi himself, and promised to be with her as soon as he could, once the will had been read. Neither of them was to know that that would take longer than anticipated...

CHAPTER EIGHT

'How the *hell* did this happen?' Adam asked Julius Beaumont's solicitor, Mark Levy. 'I told him I didn't want it.'

They were alone in the library—apart from Mervyn, they were alone in the apartment.

All the guests had gone, as well as the caterers. Henry had departed mouthing threats and obscenities. Marie-Claire had just departed; Adam had been unable to decipher her expression.

As for Mervyn, he was sitting at the kitchen table in his shirtsleeves, not quite in command of himself as he drank champagne and contemplated, with amazement, the size of the bequest he'd received.

'Julius called me out in the middle of the night a week or so ago,' Mark Levy began. 'Well, not quite the middle of the night, but late. He wanted to change his will. I tried to talk him out of doing it there and then, but he was adamant.'

'So you gave in and let him do it?' Adam suggested, with some scorn in his voice.

'Adam.' Mark rubbed his brow. 'He was entitled to leave his estate as he saw fit. And, although I let him do it, I returned several days later and assured myself he was of sound mind. He was calm and alert. He was not on any mind-altering medication. Not only did I *judge* him of sound mind, he *was* of sound mind. He *insisted* he wanted the new will to stand.'

'So it's watertight?'

Mark Levy rubbed his hands. 'I deem it to be so.'

Bridget was wearing a navy tracksuit and socks when Adam came back to her flat.

It was getting dark, and she'd turned the lamps on. To take her mind off all her demons, she'd also concocted a snow pea, prawn and chilli fettuccine. She couldn't imagine that he would be starving, and had thought that a light meal would serve best. But even as she'd cooked she'd been mentally devastated, she realised. She couldn't get out of her mind that little scene played out at the wake between Adam and Marie-Claire.

She couldn't get over the conviction that had come to her that they were made for each other. In all their turmoil, in all their conflict, there was still a *matching* between them that seemed unmistakable. And she couldn't doubt the tension she'd sensed in Adam.

Some of her mental uncertainties showed in her face. She was a little pale, and her eyes looked huge. But that was nothing to the leaden feeling in her heart…

'Hi,' she said when he came in. 'All settled?'

He took his time about replying. He shrugged out of the jacket of his dark suit, undid his black tie and opened the top couple of buttons on his white shirt. He crossed over to the stove and lifted the lid on the casserole dish containing the fettuccine. He sniffed the aroma of garlic, cloves and chilli, then looked at her rather penetratingly.

'More or less,' he said at last, as he walked back into the lounge and threw himself down in an armchair.

Bridget hesitated, suddenly aware of how

different he looked. He was also pale, and there were new lines scored beside his mouth—at least, lines she'd seen only once before. In a storm-battered shed in the Numinbah, when he'd told her some of his history...

She swallowed and poured herself a glass of water, then waved her fingers towards the fridge in unspoken query as to whether he'd like something to drink. She noticed at the same time that her engagement ring wasn't on her finger, and remembered that she'd taken it off and left it on the kitchen windowsill when she'd started to cook.

He shook his head at the drink offer, so she put her ring back on and took her water to the settee, where she sat down opposite him, with her feet tucked under her, and waited for him to go on.

'He left *you*,' he said, and dragged his fingers through his hair, 'his collection of Melbourne Cup photos.'

Bridget raised her eyebrows in genuine surprise. 'That was sweet of him.'

'Yes. He left *me* his entire holding in Beaumont Minerals.'

Bridget didn't look surprised. 'You would have expected that, wouldn't you?'

'No. I told him I didn't want it.'

'But it had to go somewhere, and if he disapproved of Henry it seems to make sense.' She shrugged, then frowned. 'Why didn't you want it? Because you didn't want anyone to think you'd been handed Beaumonts on a platter? Surely that's irrelevant now? Your uncle must have wanted you to have it.'

'It's not irrelevant,' he said irritably. 'I wanted to beat Henry fair and square. That's why.'

Bridget took a sudden breath as a kind of understanding came to her. 'Because of Marie-Claire?' she asked huskily. 'To prove to her you were better, smarter, cleverer, more powerful—whatever—than Henry?'

He raked a hand through his hair. 'Of course not.' But she could see that the tension she'd diagnosed in him in Marie-Claire's presence was still with him.

She swallowed several times, and took some deep breaths. 'Adam, I'll tell you the reason I came home this afternoon. Because your sister-in-law laid down a clear challenge to you, that's why. She's free and available. Or she will be.'

He stood up and towered over her. 'Do

you think I *want* her?' he shot back. 'Do you think I *admire* her for leaving Henry when he's fighting for his business life?'

'She could be leaving him because he's chronically unfaithful to her, by the sound of it!' Bridget returned, with some fire of her own.

They stared at each other.

Until Bridget went on, 'Anyway, those are all side issues. I think the way you want someone is printed on your heart, maybe your soul, not on a table of pros and cons. But that—that's not the only problem.'

'Go on,' he said dryly, and with a touch of weariness in his eyes—as if the last thing he needed at the moment was more homespun wisdom from her. What he wasn't to know was how all her uncertainties and fears had crystallised.

'I think,' she persevered, 'that the real problem is—as I always suspected, funnily enough—the terrible cynicism she left you with, even if you can't get her out of your heart and soul.'

'Bridget—'

'No.' She raised her hand to stop him. 'That's why I haven't been sure about marrying you. Yes, it obviously seemed like a good idea for you to marry me *at the time*.' She put her hands on her stomach. 'When this happened. And you haven't stopped pushing me into it from the day you found out, but…' She gestured helplessly and wiped away an errant tear. 'Is it the right answer for you now?'

'If I'm *pushing* you into anything—' his tone was clipped and brusque '—it's because it is a good idea. It's the best idea available to us.'

Bridget put her hands together and prayed for some inner fortitude. She looked across at him, and something struck her that seemed to make terrible sense. 'Had you heard the rumours too, Adam? About your brother and his wife? Round about the time I came back into your life?'

'What—?' He broke off. Then, 'What difference does it make?'

'It could explain a lot,' she said, out of a suddenly dry throat. 'It could explain why you were so insistent about marrying me—so surprisingly insistent. Because if you hadn't forgiven her, hadn't stopped punishing her for leaving you—'

'Bridget.' His blue gaze was supremely mocking as he broke in. 'I know you find all that water under the bridge fascinating. I knew it that night when you started to offer me advice, although you didn't know me at all,' he said moodily. 'But you're wrong.'

She raised her chin, and hauteur replaced her tearfulness. 'I don't think I am—and don't patronise me, Adam Beaumont. I think we—this baby and I,' she said, 'appealed to you as a shield, just in case you were tempted to forgive Marie-Claire and love her again.'

He brought his fist down on the arm of the chair. 'That's all nonsense, Bridget,' he said shortly.

'You may see it as such, you may believe it as such, but I don't think it is.' She got up at last and went to the window. 'There's been something holding me back, something I didn't fully understand, but now it's all clear. It's what you feel for another woman and what she still means to you. And that has to affect us.'

'Nothing can affect us,' he said brusquely. 'Except this ridiculous shillyshallying. So let's get it over and done with, Bridget. Let's do it tomorrow—in fact I won't take no for an answer.'

She gasped. 'You can't make me!'

'You're right. But I can mention the child you're carrying, whose best interests you *should* be taking into consideration.' He ground his teeth.

Bridget took a shuddery little breath, but she said tartly, 'Maybe someone should take an overall view, Adam. Marie-Claire is going to be free. For whatever reason, she's admitting she made a mistake. So you won't have to end up on your own in a wheelchair,' she added, and couldn't hide the bitterness in her voice. She turned to stare out of the window and stiffened incredulously. 'Oh, no! I don't believe it!'

He frowned. 'What?'

'M-my mother,' she stammered. 'She's just walked into the building. With a suitcase. And a taxi is driving off.' She turned back from the window, with her eyes wide and horrified and her hand to her mouth.

CHAPTER NINE

'DARLING, you mustn't upset yourself any more,' Mary Baxter, formerly Tully-Smith, said soothingly. 'This is not the end of the world.'

Bridget raised her tear-streaked face to her mother. 'How can you say that? All I've ever done is be in the wrong place at the wrong time, and that's led me into getting caught up in an absolute maelstrom of— I can't tell you how much I wish I'd never heard of the Beaumont family!'

'If only I hadn't left you to go overseas!'

'Mum, this could have happened to me if you'd lived in—in the same street.' Bridget wiped her eyes with her fingers.

'What are you going to do?' Mary asked cautiously.

Bridget propped her chin on her hands and

licked some salty tears off her lips. She'd probably never forget the awkward little scene that had ensued when she'd opened the door to her mother and received her embrace, plus her excited explanation that she had a whole week to spend with Bridget.

Then Mary had noticed Adam, and she'd started to apologise for barging in on anything, but Bridget had seen her mother's quick summing-up of Adam Beaumont as she'd introduced him, and how impressed Mary had been.

In fact she'd said as much—'What a pleasure to meet you, Adam! May I call you Adam?'

Then her eyes had fallen on Bridget's engagement ring, forgotten in all the trauma and still sitting on her daughter's left hand, and Mary had drawn a deep, deep breath.

Her next words had been, 'Is this what I think it is? But you've been so secretive, darling! Mind you, I have been away—oh, congratulations!'

Adam had been the one to find the right words.

He'd said quietly that they were engaged, but that things had got a little complicated between himself and her daughter and he knew Bridget wanted to speak to her alone. So he would leave them together but—and here he'd turned to Bridget with an unmistakable warning in his eyes—he'd be in touch tomorrow morning. And he'd left the flat, leaving her mother open-mouthed.

That was when Bridget had sunk down at the dining table in floods of tears, until she'd finally found some composure and told her mother the whole story.

'What am I going to do? I have no idea.' She sniffed and blew her nose, then reached out and pressed her mother's hand. 'Thank you for not reading me the riot act. I know you must be thinking I'm insane or something.'

'Oh, my dear.' Mary returned the pressure. 'Of course not. These things happen.'

Bridget closed her eyes. 'He doesn't love me. Adam. Well, I knew that, but I didn't know what he felt for her—not really. She was a background figure, and as such I could ignore her—more or less. Now I can't.'

'No,' Mary agreed, and surprised her daughter as she added firmly, 'Therefore the last thing you want to do is marry him.'

Bridget opened her mouth but closed it

again. 'I *am* pregnant,' she said at last, a little forlornly.

'Well,' her mother replied, 'that's going to take a bit of thinking about—but you have got me, darling! I'll be with you every step of the way.'

Uh-oh, Bridget heard herself say to herself.

She lay in bed that night and couldn't recall when she'd felt more lonely or miserable.

Yes, it was reassuring up to a point to know that her mother now knew it all, and was asleep in the spare bedroom. But how she was going to go forward, what she was going to say to Adam, were the kind of questions that resembled a secret form of torture.

Then there was the problem of her mother, even if it was reassuring to have her close by. Vague and unworldly Mary Baxter might be at times, but she could also be particularly stubborn once she set her mind on a course.

This could ruin her marriage, Bridget thought. It wouldn't be so bad if they lived here, but Jakarta was a long way away, and Richard had at least nine months of his fellowship to go. What was she going to do?

If these thoughts weren't bad enough, after she did fall into an uneasy sleep she woke and reached instinctively for Adam—and cried tears into the pillow as every time he'd made love to her came back to her. But he wasn't there. He wasn't there physically, and he wasn't there for her in any sense now. She couldn't allow him to be. Not now.

And nothing can change that, she thought. Nothing...

'Mum, I *need* to do this. Please believe me.'

It was early, about six o'clock, and cloudy, so it was grey outside and not a hopeful kind of day—which was in tune with Bridget's mood.

She'd got up to make a cup of tea, and her mother had appeared almost immediately in her favourite violet candlewick dressing gown.

'Well, I know I advised you not to marry him last night,' Mary said, 'and I stand by that. But to just disappear?' She stared at Bridget, anxiety written in her eyes.

'I need some time on my own, other-wise I might find myself getting married for entirely the wrong reasons,' Bridget said firmly—although she was feeling far from firm. She felt like a jelly inside, to be precise.

'So—what's he like? Apart from all this?' Mary queried.

Bridget stared out of the kitchen window. They were sitting with their tea at the kitchen table. 'That's the problem,' she said at last. 'He can be—' Her voice broke, but she took control. 'He can be lovely. But he can also be like a force that's impossible to resist.'

'Come with me, then,' Mary suggested. 'We'll go to Perth. That's where Richard is, with his daughter. We can both go to Perth. I know Richard will understand completely. And you can think things out there.'

'No. Thank you, Mum,' Bridget said warmly, 'but I just want to be alone for a bit. I'm not even going to tell you where I'm going, although I will be in touch, I promise. I don't really know where, but I need to go soon.'

'How soon?'

'In the next half-hour. I'm so sorry to leave you, but it's the best thing to do. Once he comes—if he comes—' She broke off.

Mary Baxter straightened. 'Let him come!

I'll deal with him! No, Bridget, I simply cannot allow you to go off on your own. If you want to, we'll go now—we'll go wherever you want—but we'll go together!'

Bridget opened her mouth, but her mother simply said, 'You're not the only one with a mind of your own, you know.' She stood up and added, 'I haven't even unpacked, so it will only take me a moment to get ready.'

Bridget spent two weeks in Perth with her mother and Richard Baxter, at his daughter's house.

The only person she'd contacted was her boss, to ask for an extension to her leave, but she hadn't given him her whereabouts.

Every time a phone rang—although she'd left her mobile in her flat—and every time someone knocked on the door of the pleasant beachside home Richard's daughter and her husband lived in, she expected it to be Adam. But it never was.

At the same time as she cursed herself for living in foolish hope, she couldn't believe it would have been that difficult to trace her movements—if he'd been so inclined.

But then she re-examined her assumption

that he could have traced her easily. Maybe not. He didn't know her mother's surname, and even if he'd found that out, and found they'd flown to Perth, once they'd arrived there, it might be like looking for a needle in a haystack, without any idea of Richard's daughter's married name, mightn't it?

As the days slid by, her warring state of mind took its toll. If anything she lost weight, and she would have given anything for the peace and serenity the baby within her must surely need.

On one hand, she was sure she was doing the right thing; on the other, there were days when she felt so alone it was frightening. And times when she was filled with a raw, yearning ache for him there seemed to be no cure for.

There was also a looming decision to be made about where to go from Perth. And what to do about her mother?

Feeling traitor-like, now they'd been in Perth for two weeks, she prompted her mother and Richard to talk about their life in Jakarta, and they gave glowing reports of it. Yes, it was a big, teeming city, but they were growing accustomed to the local customs, and the whole thing was a splendid adventure, her mother said enthusiastically.

Bridget gathered herself to say that there was no reason for them not to return to Jakarta, that she was quite able to take care of herself.

But no sooner had she shown that enthusiasm than Mary took a deep breath. She reached for Richard's hand and said, 'Darling, I think—we think—you need to go back, and you need to see Adam Beaumont and talk this through with him. Or at least communicate with him somehow. I'll come with you if you decide to see him, and Richard will advise you if you decide to do it through a lawyer.'

Bridget could only blink several times. Then she found her voice. 'But you told me not to—'

'I know,' Mary interrupted. 'But I was extremely annoyed when I first said that. To put it mildly, I could have killed him for...' Mary paused and did not elaborate. 'I'm not suggesting you marry him. But it is his baby, so he bears some responsibility for it, and for you.'

Richard Baxter cleared his throat. 'I do feel it's the best way, Bridget. And we just want you to know that, wherever you decide to be while you have this baby, we'll be there too.'

Tears misted Bridget's eyes. 'Look, that's so—so wonderful of you, but what would make me happiest is for you both to go on being happy in your new life together. Anyway, there's the fellowship and so on.'

They looked at each other, Mary and her husband, and there was so much love and confidence in the mutual decision shining in their eyes as they shrugged almost identically, as if to say *that's a minor detail*, Bridget could hardly bear the pain that slammed into her heart.

If only she and Adam had that...

'Bridget,' her mother said quietly, 'you can't only think of yourself now, sweetheart. You need some kind of stability. It's important.'

Two days later she flew back to the Gold Coast. On her own. It was the one small victory she'd achieved, although she'd promised her life on the matter of staying in touch with her mother.

It was a bright day, lovely in the sun, but with a hint of winter in the air out of it.

She looked round her flat when she got in, and found she was happy to be home. Amongst her mail there was a letter from Levy, Levy & Cartwright, who proved to be Julius Beaumont's solicitors. They were holding her bequest for her, and required her to collect it and sign for it.

She picked up her mobile phone, lying exactly where she'd left it, but of course it needed charging. She hadn't left her landline answering machine on, so her mobile was the only way Adam might have tried to contact her. But as she carried it towards the charger it slipped out of her hand and crashed to the tiled floor.

She cursed herself for being unbelievably clumsy, and bent to pick up the pieces, but the phone was now history.

Since it was late afternoon, she decided she would spend the rest of the day laying her plans and working on what she would say, both to Levy, Levy & Cartwright, and to Adam Beaumont, should she be unable to avoid him.

She went into the bedroom to unpack, and her gaze fell on her painting of the coral ixora flowers that Adam had admired, and she stopped what she was doing as memories came crowding back.

There was something else about pregnancy she was discovering, that often took her by surprise. She could and did sometimes fall asleep on the spot, and it had been a four-hour flight from Perth, with all the attendant travelling to and from airports on top of that.

Stopping only to pull her shoes off and wrap the doona around her, she slept through until early the next morning.

Anyone checking her flat for a presence, via some lights, for example, would have had no idea she was home...

'Miss Tully-Smith,' Mark Levy said the next morning in his office. 'I'm delighted to see you.'

'Thank you. Please call me Bridget. I've come to collect my pictures, and also to ask a favour of you.'

'I'm happy to help if I can, Bridget. Your pictures are boxed and ready for you. All I need is a signature.'

Bridget signed the form, then withdrew a package from her purse. 'Do you act for Adam?' she asked.

Mark Levy nodded. 'At times, but I'm not the only one. Is it—business?' he asked a shade cautiously.

'No. I just wanted this delivered to him, if you wouldn't mind.' She handed over the package. 'There's an explanatory note inside.'

Mark Levy studied her thoughtfully. He noted that although the only other time he'd met Bridget Tully-Smith she'd been wearing an engagement ring, this was no longer the case. It seemed, therefore, not unlikely that she and Adam had parted ways. In fact it wouldn't surprise him at all, he decided, if her engagement ring was in this package. Nor did she look well.

'I'll do my best, Bridget,' he said. 'But Adam is a little hard to pin down at the moment, so if it's urgent...?' He raised an eyebrow at her.

'No. Hard to pin down?' Bridget just couldn't help herself.

'I think he might be taking some time off,' Mark said. 'It will be common knowledge in the next day or two—he has ceded all his holdings in Beaumont Minerals to his brother, Henry, and since then he hasn't been around a lot.'

Bridget blinked, then stared at the solicitor, wide-eyed. 'Surely that's quite contrary to his uncle's wishes?'

Mark Levy shrugged. 'This is only my personal opinion, Bridget, but I think it's foolish to want to rule from the grave.'

'So do I, now I come to think of it,' Bridget murmured. 'But I don't understand,' she said helplessly. 'Has something happened in the family?'

Mark took his time. It *was* a known fact in the legal world that Adam had relinquished all his interests in Beaumont Minerals. What he did not know was why.

He stirred at last. 'I'm afraid I can't help you there. You haven't been in touch with Adam himself?'

Bridget cleared her throat. 'No. I was hoping…' She paused. Did it need to be a secret? 'I was hoping not to have to. Do you—would you know if Marie-Claire has gone back to Henry?'

Mark felt a pang of regret for this girl as he thought, So that's what's at the bottom of it all—for her, at least. But he could only tell her the truth. 'I believe not.'

* * *

Bridget didn't go home. She went to the beach.

She sat on a sand dune, her favourite spot, in the sun, and simply let the waves, the sunlight, the birds, and the clear blue sky soak into her psyche for a long time.

And gradually she realised why she was sitting so still, breathing it all in. It was in the hope that, just as the sea on the beach was scouring the sand clean, her dreadful confusion would be wiped away.

She put her hand on her stomach and let it lie there as she thought deeply about the baby she was carrying. Was it a boy or a girl? Would it have the Beaumont blue eyes, or green, like her own? Whatever, she reflected, the baby was her absolute priority now. And, whatever, nothing could change who this baby's father was. And, since they couldn't live together in harmony, some kind of arrangement had to be made. Not in anger, though.

But what had happened to make Adam relinquish his desire to take control of Beaumont Minerals? Yes, he hadn't wanted to get there on his uncle's coattails, so to speak, or on anyone's. But a legitimate bequest, his uncle's dying wish, had to be another matter, surely?

And as she thought about it, she realised she'd believed that he would see it that way eventually. She'd believed that over and above herself and the baby, even over and above Marie-Claire, that was what meant most to Adam Beaumont: control of Beaumont Minerals. It was the only thing that would redress not only Marie-Claire's defection and Henry's perfidy, but his father's treatment of him.

So what to make of this news?

She picked up a handful of sand and let it drift through her fingers. It could have no bearing on her, though. And she thought of the note she'd written and put into the package with his engagement ring.

I'm happy to make some arrange-ment, not marriage, but an arrange-ment, whereby we live our separate lives but your child has your protection and love.

She'd penned a final line:

This is not negotiable.

Tears blurred her eyes and a song came into her heart. The Dolly Parton song Whitney Houston had made even more famous—'I Will Always Love You'…

Her tears had dried, and she was staring out to sea following a yacht sailing south when she decided it was time to go home.

She got up and brushed herself off, but she was still thinking of Adam Beaumont as she came to the road and stepped off the pavement—almost under the wheels of a car.

Someone saved her. Someone with a strong pair of arms pulled her away in the nick of time. And that someone was furiously angry.

Adam, who'd never looked taller, in jeans and a navy sweater, or more threatening.

'How can you just step onto a road without checking the traffic?' he ground out. 'How can you be so foolish? Don't you know I've scoured the length and breadth of the country looking for you? And the moment I find you, you're about to wipe yourself out!'

His eyes blazed down at her and his mouth worked, then he pulled her into his arms and held her so tight she could barely breathe. Not only that, she could feel the heavy, slamming beat of his heart, and she couldn't doubt there was fear as well as anger driving him.

'Adam—Adam…' she whispered. 'I didn't think you cared—'

'Cared!' He held her a little away from him and stared at her.

'No.'

'Well, you're wrong,' he said shortly, then visibly took hold of himself. 'I'm sorry. You gave me a fright.'

Bridget swallowed. 'Who…how did you find me? Or is it just coincidence?'

'Yes and no.' He released her, but took her hand. 'Can we go back to the beach?'

She nodded after a moment.

He said no more until they'd reached the beach. 'I called in to see Mark Levy, so I knew you were back in town, and I got your note. You weren't home, so I— We used to come here together sometimes, remember?'

'Y-yes,' she stammered. 'Adam—' she couldn't help herself '—why did you let Beaumonts go? I thought it meant more to you than anything.'

'To prove to you I could live without anything, but not without you.'

Bridget stared at him with her lips parted and her eyes huge.

He rubbed his jaw. 'I know you may find it hard to believe after our last encounter, but when I discovered that I might never find you, that I didn't even know where to start looking, sanity kicked in—and I couldn't believe I'd been such a bloody fool. I couldn't believe I hadn't realised until then how much I loved you, and hadn't made you believe it.'

She tried to speak, but no words came.

'Where were you, incidentally?'

'Perth.' She explained about her mother.

He grimaced. 'You may not realise it, but there are two private detective agencies trying to track you down.' He sketched a smile, but it didn't reach his eyes. 'Because once that revelation hit me I knew I had to get you back.'

'So…' She had trouble making her voice work. 'But to walk away from Beaumonts…?'

He took her hand. 'Sit down.'

They sat down, side by side.

'I have no regrets,' he said, and paused, almost as if he was looking back down the path of his life. 'Beaumonts has been a torment, a real thorn in my flesh, ever since I can remember,' he said slowly, and stared out to sea. Then he turned back to her. 'Not only that, but it led me into making the worst mistake of my life.'

'Marie-Claire?' she hazarded, and held her breath.

'Yes. She epitomises all the blunders I've made in the name of believing I had some right to the company.'

He hesitated and seemed to gather his thoughts. 'It wasn't only that she left me for Henry, it was the fact that she really left me for Beaumonts that made me so bitter and so hellbent on revenge. You were right about the cynicism she left me with—' He broke off and looked tortured. 'And you were right again. You and our baby *did* seem like a good way to keep her at bay, keep on punishing her. It was only looking back after you'd gone, when I remembered all my days in the sun with you.' He stopped. 'Anyway, it was only then that I saw what I'd been too blind to see—too wrapped up in my own ambitions, too wrapped up in all my old scars, going way back to my father. Marie-Claire meant nothing to me any more, and neither did Beaumonts. I *loved you.*'

Bridget moved her hands and discovered she had tears rolling down her cheeks.

'I didn't mean to make you sad.'

'I—I—I'm still amazed, though,' she confessed. 'You believed, and your uncle Julius believed, Henry wasn't doing a good job.'

Adam heaved a sigh. 'Henry,' he said, 'has his own demons. He's had me breathing down the back of his neck for years, watching every step he made. And he's had Marie-Claire manipulating him— I know he's been no saint in that direction but, well, things could change now. Anyway, it's no concern of mine. I've been a basket case since you left,' he went on. 'I can't seem to function without you. My staff are in despair because I'm never there, and I never know where I'm liable to be either.'

Bridget smiled a trembling little smile. 'Where have you been?'

'Chasing up leads on you, Mrs Smith. Hang on! I drove past your apartment last night but there wasn't a single, solitary light—when did you get home?'

She told him, and explained about the lack of lights too.

'Well, at least you got my demented messages on your mobile phone. Or—did you?'

Bridget shook her head. 'I didn't. I dropped my phone and smashed it before I could charge it.'

He swore under his breath, but there was a glint of humour in his eyes. He was silent for a long moment, then, 'Do you believe me, Bridget?' He stared deep into her eyes. 'You once said to me that if I needed you I knew where to find you—I need you with every fibre of my being.'

Bridget thought of what he'd given away, how he'd changed his life for her. She thought of his reaction to her all but stepping in the path of a car. 'Yes.'

'And—am I forgiven?'

She breathed in the very essence of him and felt her senses come alive. 'Oh, yes...'

He hesitated, as if he couldn't quite believe her soft avowal, then he swept her into his arms.

Some minutes later they became aware of a little boy of about six, standing nearby and watching them closely.

'What are you doing?' he asked.

Bridget released herself from Adam's arms and patted herself down self-consciously.

'I was kissing this lady,' Adam said gravely.

'Is she your mother?'

Bridget made a strangled sort of noise.

'No, but she's going to be my wife.'

'Oh. I only kiss my mother,' the boy asserted. 'My dad and I shake hands. Well, sometimes I kiss my grandmother, but she hugs me almost to death so I don't really like it.'

'I don't blame you. Uh—are you on your own, young man?' Adam enquired.

The boy swung round and pointed to a couple at the water's edge. 'I s'pose I better go back. They don't like me to wander away. Bye!' He ran off.

'Do I *look* like your mother?' Bridget enquired.

He smiled down into her eyes. 'No, you don't, Mrs Smith. And I also have to tell you that this beach is far too public for us.'

'And I have to tell you—' her lips curved '—I agree with you.'

'Your place or mine?' he asked quizzically.

'Mine is closer,' she said demurely.

'So be it. Race you?' he teased.

'No, you can drive me.'

But they were serious again as they lay in each other's arms in her bed.

'I can't quite believe I deserve this.' He ran his hand down her body, then rested it on her belly.

She looked into his eyes and saw they were sombre. 'I think I've always loved you,' she said quietly. 'One of the reasons I was so unsure about marrying you was because I didn't just want respect, care and affection from you. I wanted you to love me the way I love you.'

He closed his eyes. 'I can't believe I was such a fool.'

'Hush,' she recommended. 'We've got a whole new life in front of us. And I'm dying that special kind of death again. Are you?'

He groaned, and everything he did to her from then on showed unequivocally that he was...

They were married two weeks later.

It was small, simple and private, but the

bride glowed in a strapless cream silk dress, and wore an emerald pendant to match her engagement ring.

The bride's mother, who had forgiven Adam Beaumont, was also radiant.

And in the fullness of time Adam and Bridget were blessed with a daughter they named Grace Mary. She had her mother's coppery hair and her father's blue eyes. This called for another celebration—a christening.

When the guests had departed, and Mount Grace was quiet and settled for the night, Bridget said to Adam, 'Your daughter requires your presence.'

He looked up. He was sitting on the chintzy settee in the lounge with his feet up, surrounded by the weekend papers. 'Since my daughter is only three months old and cannot talk, how did she indicate this to you?'

'I can tell.' Bridget had changed from her christening finery into slim cream pants and a green blouse, which she happened to be buttoning up.

'Here.' He got up. 'Let me—you've got them crooked.'

She accepted his ministrations, and her lips

curved as he patted her down and murmured, 'All present and correct. For the moment.'

She looked into his blue eyes and deduced, correctly, that he would be undressing her in the not too distant future. And she was shaken inwardly by how much she loved Adam Beaumont; how, after all the trauma, the joy of being married to him never left her.

She was still, at times, amazed at the change in him—wrought by freeing himself from the yoke of his bitterness, and helped by their closeness. There were no longer two men in her life, just the one Adam Beaumont—the one she'd loved right from the start.

She slipped her arms around his neck. 'Do you ever think of that night in the Numinbah?'

'Yes. Do you?'

'I do,' she concurred gravely. 'I used to think that it was the most foolish act of my life, to sleep with a man I'd never met before because I thought I was going to die. But I don't think it's turned out to be such a bad thing after all.'

'Ah. One could even say you showed not only great judgement but great taste,' he offered, with a perfectly straight face.

Bridget looked at him in mock disapproval, then had to laugh. 'Don't get too swollen a head,' she warned, all the same.

'Why would I do that?'

'Since you have not one but two adoring females in your life, it's quite possible. Now, Grace won't go to sleep until she sees you. Trust me. I know this.'

He laughed and kissed her lightly. 'I don't believe you for a moment, but I'll come—in a moment.'

She raised her eyebrows at him.

'It's simple,' he said. 'All I want to say is—I love you. The only problem is I keep on wanting to say it, over and over.' His blue eyes were quite serious.

Bridget melted against him. 'It's not a problem,' she assured him.